Euan followed the scent into the trees,

realising that his prey was more aware, cannier, than he had expected. The trail was easy to follow for Euan, with his sensitive sense of smell, but without that he would have lost the man quickly. He seemed to have moved swiftly but surely through the trees, following the trails left by deer and other wildlife.

Euan groaned as the sound of running water grew stronger. This hunt was suddenly going to get a whole lot harder. It was a matter of honour now. Giving up was not an option for him. The wolf inside bared its teeth in a smile at the challenge. Euan reached the water, crouching to slip a hand in, feeling the chill melt water run through his fingers. He cast about both up and down stream but he knew that his prey has crossed the water, probably wading through it for a while before moving up the far bank. It's what he would have done.

Euan smiled, eyes crinkling at the corners. Finally, someone would make him work for his prize.

Also recommended...

You may also enjoy these other ForbiddenFiction works:

Red and the Wolf by Kailin Morgan

Aidan is content. He's got a good job, nice house and is comfortable in the small town — far away from anyone who knows his secrets. Yet, he feels the prickle of something stalking him. It doesn't help when a stranger starts insinuating his way into Aidan's life. Newcomer Seth is attractive in a way that stirs something in Aidan he had thought long buried. Can he keep his secret and continue in his solitary life or will events conspire against him to drag the truth into the light and change everything? (M/M)

http://forbiddenfiction.com/library/story/KM1-1.000104

His Whipping Boy by J.A. Jaken

Cedric de Breos was from an average farmer's family before he was chosen — by royal decree — to befriend Alain Tomolia, the solemn and enigmatic crown prince of Dunn. As Cedric dutifully pursues their strange friendship, he notices that Alain is haunted by a dark secret, one with its roots sunk deep in the crown prince's past. Cedric also discovers that his intended purpose is not only to serve as companion to the crown prince but also as his surrogate in the whipping yard, taking the punishment for Alain's misdeeds. Will Cedric find a way to come to terms with the resentment, pity, curiosity, and reluctant attraction he feels toward the crown prince, or will he allow the circumstances around them to command their fate? (M/M)

http://forbiddenfiction.com/library/story/JAJ-1.000182

His Highland Wolf

Kailin Morgan

ForbiddenFiction
www.forbiddenfiction.com

an imprint of

Fantastic Fiction Publishing
www.fantasticfictionpublishing.com

HIS HIGHLAND WOLF
A Forbidden Fiction book

Fantastic Fiction Publishing
Hayward, California

© Kailin Morgan, 2014

CREDITS
Editor: James L. Wolf and D.M. Atkins
Cover Design: Siolnatine
Cover Art: Jeannie Bell
Production Editor: Erika L Firanc
Proofreading: Kaye O'Malley

SKU: KM1-000142-02 FFP
ISBN: 978-1-62234-156-6

Published in the United States of America

DISCLAIMER

This book is a work of fiction which contains explicit erotic content; it is intended for mature readers. Do not read this if it's not legal for you.

All the characters, locations and events herein are fictional. While elements of existing locations or historical characters or events may be used fictitiously, any resemblance to actual people, places or events is coincidental.

This story is not intended to be used as an instruction manual. It may contain descriptions of erotic acts that are immoral, illegal, or unsafe. Do not take the events in this story as proof of the plausibility or safety of any particular practice.

Contents

Chapter 1
Night Descends

Thick clouds slid across the pale crescent moon. If the men didn't know this area well, a single step could be fatal as they made their way across the ridge above the small loch. Euan, the leader of the little group, paused for a second, crouched on the edge of the ridge, studying the progress of the line of bobbing lights making their way round the side of the loch below. The moon gave the earth a final glimpse of her pale face, the clouds parting briefly, the soft light glistening on the dark blond hair that fell across Euan's high cheekbones. His gaze flicked briefly skywards as the moon was swallowed up before he concealed himself in the shadows with the rest of his clan.

Euan signalled his men to gather around him, waiting until they were all crouched in a tight huddle.

"Lachlan," Euan said softly, deep voice barely carrying on the still night air. Lachlan, one of the more scrawny looking men, nodded his acknowledgement to Euan. "Take Niall and Connor with ye, take out the rear guard. Rest of ye are with me, we'll take them once they pass the copse, there's a wee bend in the path there, keep us nice and hidden. Barn owl says go." Nods and sharp grins went round the circle as arrows were checked for a final time and knives were drawn, the blades darkened with soot to avoid catching any stray glimmers of light. Soft and silent as shadows, Euan's men made their way down the hillside to take up their positions surrounding the road below. Several owl hoots rang out in the night as the men signalled they were in position.

Tristan felt the hard wood of the side of the cart press into his ribs as he stared into the night. Following the shore of the loch a long, bedraggled line of people trailed slowly through the darkness behind the cart, the flickering, smoky torches some of them carried doing little to show them the uneven ground underfoot. Tristan had seen many of them stumble or fall and several horses were already showing signs of going lame after catching their hooves in the tough clumps of heather that grew at the sides of the road. Their riders now walked beside them, leading them carefully. The line had closed up as dusk had darkened in to night, the travellers huddling together for comfort as they journeyed through the unknown countryside.

Lord Barnard, the nobleman in the charge of the group, had been forced into the cart beside Tristan and the other more favoured servants after his charger had broken a leg in a rabbit hole that morning. It had been startled by a pheasant that had flown from its hiding place in the bracken at the side of the track.

Tristan had watched silently as Lord Barnard had made one of the guards slaughter the horse. He knew that his lord had felt it a sad waste. Lord Barnard had been somewhat fond of the beast but the horse would have been of no use to them. There was nothing they could have done for it, and they had left the corpse at the side of the track. Now his lord travelled in the back of a wooden cart, robes wrapped tight around his stout figure. Tristan knew that it wasn't how he had wanted to appear, but then he hadn't wanted to travel north at all, to this nest of raiders and reivers. The country was barely civilised in Lord Barnard's opinion, which he had expressed loudly and at length to any of the servants in earshot.

The political situation had been uncertain for the past couple of years as lords fought for the favours of the new king. There had been many tussles over strategic stretches of land as the king began to parcel pieces up as bribes to the new Scottish gentry. And, as the new king was the king of both England and Scotland, he had sent Lord Barnard north to work on trade agreements and to see what else the man could find out in a bid to bring the errant Scots to heel. Information gathering was also Tristan's job.

"Dammit man! D'ye think I want your foul stench anywhere near me?" the lord cursed as a rut in the road caused all aboard to tumble over. The lord's temper was short at the best of times, and was almost volcanic now.

"I... I... p-p-please forgive me m'lord," the cook stammered his apology as he vainly tried to shift his bulk in the small cart.

"I should've left you at the side of the road with my horse," grunted Lord Barnard. "Would've, if only me damn wife hadn't taken to your cooking so much." This group was the second wave of a move north. Servants had already been sent on ahead to make the new keep as habitable as possible for the new lord. His wife and her servants would be moving north in a couple of weeks, once she had been delivered of her child.

Tristan motioned to the cook to take his place as he slipped nimbly over the side of the slow-moving vehicle and went to join the rest of those walking along behind. His body was still filling out and he hadn't taken up much space, but in the cramped confines of the cart, every inch mattered. He pushed his dark hair back from his face before his slender fingers checked, almost unconsciously, that the small satchel was still over his shoulder, tucked carefully under his cloak. It did not matter that he didn't know what it contained, just that it made its way safely to its destination.

Although Lord Barnard was the richest man in the party, it was the slender, dark haired figure that was most important.

A nightingale let out a quiet trill as the bobbing lights approached a small copse of bushes where the loch edged closer to the road. As the guards at the front of the group of travellers walked through, one of them, slightly more alert than his companions, paused briefly at the sound of an owl's hoot, but tiredness had dulled his senses and he was too late to raise the alarm before his life was taken by a silent arrow in the night. As the rest of the group came out the other side, it was too late for them. Bridles were grabbed and the horses drooped to a weary stop.

"I did not order a stop!" boomed the lord's voice, the echoes carrying across the dark, still waters.

"Aye, that may be so. But you're no longer in charge."

Euan stepped out from the shadows into the blossoming torch-light, green eyes fixed on Lord Barnard's jowled face. He smiled, the sight more threatening than welcoming. "I think you'll find that your days of making orders are about to run out." He didn't introduce himself. The less this group of English invaders knew about his group of men the better as far as Euan was concerned. Any lord was bad news in Euan's opinion, but the English were worse; absent Lairds with no idea what was happening to the people trying to eke a living from the land, only interested in the money coming in from the estates or the occasional hunting trip.

"Guards! Guards?" The heavyset lord looked around, face ruddy with impotent rage as his calls remained unanswered.

"Ye mean these guards?" asked Euan with a slight curl of his lips, as he pointed to the group of men, already bound, huddled at the side of the lake. Lord Barnard spluttered and fell silent, as if he was realising that he would just have to go along with this brigand until he found out what it was Euan wanted. Euan watched, amused, as the portly lord started to stand, ready no doubt to declare to this petty criminal exactly who he was when Euan just turned away from him and spoke into the darkness.

"Right lads, move them out." Men appeared like ghosts out of the surrounding bushes, taking up the places of the old guards. The guards had been prodded to their feet; a long rope linked them together and this was then fastened to the back of the cart. A whip cracked over the heads of the horses and slowly the group moved off down the trail again, and Lord Barnard subsided back into his furs with a low murmur. Perhaps he had realised that there was only one reason for this capture, and it would not serve him well to start an argument when perhaps more persuasive methods would bring a better result. Euan sighed in relief. A cooperative captive would make everything easier.

The sky began to lighten in the east, bringing shades of grey to the dark countryside. As the first sliver of sun appeared on the horizon, the cart was brought to a halt. Everyone piled up behind with sighs and groans issuing from their throats as muscles twinged and protested over the long, forced march.

"Lachlan, ye know what needs doing," murmured Euan. One of

his men jogged over to a cairn at the side of the road and, after digging around behind it, he produced a large bundle of dark, heavy wool. As he approached the cart he signalled to a couple of the other Scots to come join him.

"Right, everyone out! Come on, all of ye out!"

As the group struggled out of the cart, their hands were bound behind them and their eyes covered with the heavy wool. It hadn't been worthwhile making them do this before as they had needed their prisoners to walk, but now they were close enough to transport them the remaining distance to their camp in a couple of trips on the back of the wagons. All the cases and trunks and boxes were dumped at the side of the road. They would come back for them later and pick through them for what could be used, resold or melted down.

Tristan had noticed Lord Barnard's anxious glance, but he had already removed his markers of rank, tucking them into his satchel before he slicked his hair back, tying it with a narrow strip of ribbon. It made him look completely different, his fine features revealed. He looked more like a clerk, young, thin and unlikely to be any trouble. The man who approached him seemed to think that way too. Tristan shivered as the dark wool was wrapped over his eyes, but he comforted himself with the fact that they had not yet found his bag, tucked under his shirt as it was. He would have to find somewhere to hide the small satchel though, before they found out what it carried.

At least the more important secrets were carried inside his head, and they would be unable to search there. Tristan had shown a natural aptitude for remembering the epic poems and tales that were used to pass down history and laws in the small community he came from. This talent had been spotted by the local minister, who had then brought it to the attention of the duke. Tristan had been taken from his home, his family, without notice or choice and his new life had begun.

His sensitive ears picked up the sounds of people being pushed back up into the newly emptied carts, then the sound of the first of them moving off down a track towards the west. Tristan blinked, feeling his eyelashes brush against the coarse wool. If he looked straight down, he could see a tiny sliver of ground beneath his feet. He moved away from the dusty road surface taking small, careful sidesteps until the dirt under his feet became grass. Tristan dropped to the ground while trying to make himself as small and unnoticeable as possible.

"Right, the rest of ye, up onto the cart, and settle yerself down. Nae complaints from any of ye, we're no doing this for yer comfort."

That's Lachlan, Tris thought to himself. *Seems to be the group's second-in-command.* He listened carefully to any exchanges he could overhear, trying to build up an idea of who it was that had captured the group. It was most likely a group of brigands seeking ransom for what they thought would be an important lord.

"Up ye get." The voice came out of nowhere, startling Tris from his thoughts, and he jumped slightly.

"Come on, up on your feet. Ye cannae hide from us, lad."

The sound of people being prodded and pulled to their feet filled the air to be followed by bumps, curses and yelps as they were pushed and shoved into the carts. Tris followed the instructions given, as he picked his way carefully across the uneven surface, and allowed himself to be manhandled up into one of the carts.

"That's all o' them," said a man Tris had named Frog due to his thin, croaking voice.

"Niall, Connor, you're on clean-up and guard duty here, Euan will send the carts back for the goods worth keeping," said Lachlan. "The rest of you, come with us. Maeve said that there would be fresh bread today."

"Just so long as ye leave us some," yelled Niall over the sound of the departing carts.

Tris listened carefully, making mental notes of all the sounds he could hear and the way the carts tipped either left or right as they turned. As the only one of the lord's servants with any appreciable skills at writing, and with his connections to the Church, it would be his job to make an escape and try to bring help. He could hear the noises of an encampment swelling, becoming more distinct. The smell of baking breads filtered its way through the greener scents of pine and heather. The carts ground to a halt, horses whinnied and stamped as they were unharnessed, wood creaked as people were unloaded, curses and yelps ringing out once again.

"Your turn now, lad." ordered Lachlan, placing a callused palm under Tris's elbow to guide him to the edge of the cart. As he dropped down, Lachlan removed the wool covering his face, but left his hands bound.

They had been brought to a small, fortified camp. The natural growths of brambles, bindweed and nettles had been encouraged to sprout between the trees surrounding three-quarters of the camp. *No way out there*, thought Tris, *unless I become a squirrel*. Several small huts, made from wood and sod, backed up against the trees, provided shelter from the weather and cook fires burned in front of them.

Tris flicked a glance to the other side of the camp, where the horses were being led back down the track. A ditch was followed by a row of sharpened stakes, with only a narrow opening that allowed the track to pass through. The breeze wafted back into Tris's face, bringing a stench of piss and other less identifiable scents.

"Try and avoid the ditch, then," he said to himself.

Moving with the rest of the captives, he shuffled over to a hastily fenced off area, where their hands were loosened before they were pushed into the stockade. Tris hid himself amidst the crowd. He watched carefully as Euan approached. The man's green eyes flashed almost gleefully as he surveyed the group. Tris hunched in on himself under his cloak, hiding his height. He moved behind the heavyset cook to give himself a place to observe Euan without being directly observed himself.

Tris took his time looking. *This is only because I must be able to describe him*, he told himself. *Not because he is so... attractive*. Euan's figure was well-muscled, taller than Lord Barnard, taller even than Tris. His soft brown hair was shorter than most of the other soldiers here, blond glints showing in the pale autumn sunshine and he was close shaven, a hint of reddish brown scruff shading his jaw line. Euan, like most of the other Scots, was clothed in a loose, undyed linen shirt with wide sleeves hiding the musculature underneath. Tris's gaze travelled lower to where a length of heavy wool was wrapped round Euan's trim waist, held in place with a wide belt. One end of the wool strip was pulled through the belt and draped up over his left shoulder. Hose kept his lower legs warm; simple shoes protected his feet from the chill earth.

Having spent his childhood in the North of England, Tris hadn't seen men actually dressed in kilts before, and he had to admit that the sight was much better than he had expected.

"My lord! Why don't ye make your way over here, so that we can have a wee chat?"

Although Euan had phrased it as a question, his tone of voice let the lord know that there was only one real answer. Lord Barnard stalked over, his haughty manner somewhat spoiled by the mud coating his fine cloak, clotting the fur trim into ragged lumps, and the fact that his high boots were unsuitable for walking.

Lord Barnard and Euan disappeared into one of the small huts. Lachlan followed after, carrying a wineskin and a platter of fresh bread. Tris cursed softly to himself, knowing he had no chance of finding out what was happening in there. He made himself as comfortable as possible on the damp ground and worked on his plan for escape.

Once his lord returned, Tris casually wandered over to see if he had anything to pass on. Lord Barnard didn't seem too distressed so Tris supposed that there would be a ransom demand for the group rather than wholesale slaughter. His lord leaned close to speak quietly to the young bard, careful to keep his voice low so he wouldn't be overheard.

"They're going to hold us to ransom, Tristan. A messenger is being sent out at first light. You need to be on your way before then. If you can make your way to the keep, do so, and let Sir Christopher know where we were and what has happened. If he is not there you will have to try and make your way back to York, to the Church. Take this with you." Lord Barnard reached into the padded front of his breeches and removed a small bundle of letters. He gave a small shrug at Tristan's raised eyebrow.

"Twas the only place I could think to hide them at such short notice. I did not suppose they would think to strip me."

Tris slipped the letters into his satchel, nodded his understanding of his lord's plan, his gaze finding Euan again as he strode around the camp. Euan stopped to speak to a fair number of his men, calling them all by name or some diminutive. It looked like he cared about their welfare, smiling as a small child ran behind him in some form of game. This interest from a leader was unusual to Tris. After Tris had been noticed by his local lord, he had been taken from his family, moved into the local monastery, and taught how to write in both Latin and the common tongue. At no point had anyone seemed to care about what the loss of a son would have done to his family or what the loss of his family would do to him. All they had been interested in was what they could get Tristan to do for them.

From there he had moved into the service of the duke although the Church had kept a firm grip on him, using him to gather information on issues that may have affected them. Now here he was travelling north, supposedly as Lord Barnard's spy, although there were other tasks he was to accomplish along the way. Lord Barnard had no idea that Tris had been placed with him because of his lower standing in Court society. A standing that had become more precarious due to a rather unfortunate gambling habit, hence the move to this new estate, which would hopefully remove Lord Barnard from temptation.

Tris watched as Euan shared a brief moment with Lachlan. They shared a smile and a laugh and Tris wondered if they had been friends a long time. Their friendship obviously gave Lachlan the freedom to disagree with his commander as he shook his head when Euan indicated towards the prisoners. Euan cut Lachlan's words off with a sharp gesture and a tilt of his head towards the group and stalked away. Tris considered whether their friendship made it easier or harder to give and take orders. After a moment Lachlan's shoulders drooped in what Tris imagined was a sigh of surrender. Water jugs were passed round the prisoners along with lumps of bread soaked in thin gravy. Judging by Lachlan's scowl, he wasn't happy about giving in, but had enough grace to follow a direct order.

Night fell quickly, as the sun passed behind the trees, and the sky darkened further with heavy cloud. It had been a long, boring day of captivity but it had allowed Tris to consider his escape well. He tucked his satchel deeper under his muddy cloak and made his way over to the fence. A guard looked over and Tris made signs that he was just relieving himself. As the guard looked away, Tris raised his hands to one of the heavy poles and took a deep breath. He would only get one shot at this. He bunched his muscles and leapt up and over the fence landing in a crouch on the other side. Watching the guards carefully, he made his way behind a group of small shelters, then rose up and stretched. Sometimes the best place to hide was in plain sight. He huddled his cloak round himself, pulling his hood down to shadow his face and shuffled towards the gate.

The guards on duty looked up from their game of dice. "I'm away for a piss," Tris said before they could ask. His voice was croaked like the man he'd named Frog. "Fecking cold goes right though ye, eh?"

"Aye, yer no wrong. Dinnae be too long out there. Malcolm said he heard wolves out there the other night."

Once Tris reached the edge of the tree line he carefully glanced back, his hands apparently busy at the front of his cloak. The guards were facing into the camp, watching a young girl walking towards them with a couple of bowls and a small loaf of bread. Tris took his chance, disappearing swiftly amongst the trunks. He worked his way through the trees as silently as he could, trying to keep parallel to where he thought the road was.

Tris kept count of the time by reciting poetry in his head. He knew the exact length of time each poem took and once he had been fighting his way through the undergrowth for half an hour he thought it safe to head back towards the road. He only hoped he could find it. He had been trying as best as he could to keep in a straight line, but trees did not grow in an orderly fashion and several times he had been forced to travel round thicker patches of undergrowth.

Just then the moon slid out from behind the clouds, as if to aid him and Tris could see the trees thinning out to his left. Just as he was about to set foot on to the rutted dirt of the road he heard a soft crack. He melted against the trunk to the side of him and glanced around, the moon flickering on a shadowy shape moving through the trees just where Tris had been heading. Almost without thinking he turned back into the forest and moved as swiftly and silently through the trees as he could until he spotted what he wanted. He had been expecting a chase but hadn't thought that the Scots would send out a man so quickly.

Tris held his breath, pressed flat against the wide branch of the beech tree he had clambered up. He was only a couple of feet above Euan's head, watching as he moved silently below. But it seemed fate was on his side tonight and Euan moved off into the forest. Knowing that Euan could still be out on the road or that other men could come along, Tris remained on the branch for an hour before clambering down and making his way back to the loch side to continue the journey towards Lord Barnard's keep.

Chapter 2
The Wild Hunt

Two days later, Euan found himself curled on a branch, edged as close to the trunk of the oak as he could get, trying to stay hidden in the shadows cast by the branches spreading above. It occurred to him then that this was probably what that young lad had done. Euan pictured him finding a tree and hoisting himself up. The dark would have helped to conceal him and he had probably watched Euan trailing through the forest beneath him.

He wondered if the boy had known he was being followed or if he had been alerted by Euan's misstep when a bat swooped past his face. It was obvious the boy was more than he had appeared, but how much more? Not that it mattered now. At least the young man had got away, since it didn't look like Euan or any of his men were going to. He was the last of the hunting party: Ruaridh, Connor, Bran, Niall, they were all gone. Euan tried to put the puzzle together, images flipping through his mind as the story played itself out in his memory.

They had celebrated the successful kidnapping, but reality had hit all too soon. The prisoners would need some kind of food; the captured group more than doubling their numbers. It was only right that the king supplied the meat to keep his loyal subjects, knowingly or not. Euan and some of his best men had gone hunting, poaching really, if truth be told. They had risen early, dressing and arming themselves as dawn had just begun to streak the sky with shades of pink, and before long they had been deep in the forest, tracking a deer.

Why this small group of men had come to follow Euan, he had no idea. He was the second son of an outcast and murdered Highland chieftain. Euan had no money and no land. Even his name was of no good to his men. It was more than likely to get them killed in certain circles to be truthful; but still, he had kept them alive and kept them safe so far. But, even here on the outskirts of society, times were changing. The king had left his pleasure seeking behind, and turned to the Church. Some said he was taking his piety too far. The witch hunts had started again and he seemed convinced that Scotland was breeding malcontents and others who would betray him or wished to stand against him.

Soldiers had become more common. Hunting parties made up of rich noblemen, up from England to hunt the plentiful game birds, ventured out from the cities. Land was offered to them for their loyalty. Euan's small group had been forced further into the countryside after villagers had turned on one of their women, when she tried to trade eggs for flour. They had drowned her in the pond, after a woman had accused her of leading her husband astray and curdling the cow's milk in its belly.

Now they were desperate. The children's ribs pushed stark against their grubby skin and all the adults were eating less to try and feed them. The women were making do with what roots and greenery they could scrabble during the summer months. But they had nowhere to farm, and barely enough room to provide forage for the chickens they had stolen, and plants were thin on the ground during the cold months. A deer would keep them for a fortnight at least if they eked it out with broth and the dried roots and fruits they had managed to store. But with the extra mouths they would need to find two, or hopefully three, healthy animals.

They'd stumbled on a fresh kill with blood still spilling slick from the torn out throat, and the copper-iron scent heavy in the air. Euan had raised a hand, signalling his men to halt behind him so they would stay mostly hidden in the trees. It wasn't like hunters to leave a carcass; something else had been the cause of this. Then, out from the shadows of the trunks across the clearing, it had come; fur thick and dark, muzzle stained and sticky with blood. The wolf had stalked forward, and dropped its head to sniff almost disinterestedly at the fallen deer, before it turned its dark eyes back to the men frozen in front of it.

Euan had been hunting these woods for years. He had come across the tracks of wolves before, or the occasional head attached to a post in a farmer's field, a warning to the wolves that they would not be tolerated. But he had never had a wolf approach him, and stare at him this brazenly. It was obviously well-fed with muscles heavy under the grey flecked ruff that covered its shoulders. He felt his men shuffle nervously behind him before he felt a slight push as Bran stepped forward, moving them all further into the clearing.

"Lord's sake..." Euan wanted to turn to Bran, and find out why he couldn't stay put as he had been told, but he couldn't take his eyes from the beast in front of him. He could almost swear the wolf was smiling at him, with pink tinged saliva drooling from one corner of its jaw.

"Euan." Bran's voice was tremulous, almost a whisper. "Euan, I think they're hunting us, too."

This time Euan did turn around. "Dinnae be daft Bran, one weird wolf I can understand, but dinnae be telling me that there are wolves hunting..." His words trailed off as he spotted the other two wolves slinking slowly out of the trees behind them. One was smaller. Euan thought that it could be female, but there was no way he was interested in getting close enough to find out.

He turned slowly back to the first wolf, who was still next to the deer that was obviously the pack's kill. Raising his hands, Euan gestured slightly with his fingers, and his men fanned out to either side, ready to slip away into the trees. Keeping his gaze moving from wolf to trees and off to the side, he tried to slip sideways.

"Sorry. Didnae realise we were poaching." Euan didn't know why he was talking to the wolf, but there was a dark intelligence behind those amber eyes. He continued speaking, keeping his voice low and reassuring. "Me and my men, we'll just head off this way, no need to be getting into any trouble..."

The wolf snorted, sounding, strangely, amused, if wolves could be amused.. Euan blinked and felt Niall slide past behind him. Then the wolf shook its head from side to side, looking past Euan to the two wolves behind them, exposing sharp white teeth as a low growl rumbled from its throat.

"Shite! Run! Up a tree if you can lads!" Euan heard rather than saw his men scatter to the sides, heard a low bark from the wolves behind, followed by a short howl from the wolf in front, but he was already darting through the trees, following the swiftly moving Niall.

A sudden yell split the air. *Bran*, Euan thought. The yell escalated into a howl of pain, before the sound cut off abruptly. Another dull thud and a wet crunch sounded off to one side. Euan knew it would have been either Ruaridh or Connor. Euan turned a sharp left, feeling the hot brush of breath and the tickle of fur against his leg, hearing the scrabble of paws in the leaf litter as the wolf turned to continue the chase.

He heard the sound of Connor cursing off to one side, and could see Niall darting through the trees in front while looking desperately for one with low enough branches to get them off the ground. Euan darted off down a faint trail, moving away from Connor and Niall. Another scream ripped through the still of the forest dawn, a plea to the gods, to whomever was listening, but no-one was. Euan let his eyes close for a brief second, wishing Connor's soul safe passage.

Then, there it was, looming out of the greyness of the dawn, salvation. A broad oak stood sentinel over its circle of woodland, with branches swinging low towards the earth. Lungs heaving, muscles pushing past their limits, Euan leapt and pulled himself up onto one of the broad branches. He hoisted himself up higher and huddled into the shadow of the trunk. He could feel the damp warmth of blood trickling down his left leg, and the scratches of bramble beginning to sting as the flood of fear that had rushed through him bottomed out and left him shaking and pale.

He clutched at the tree, frozen for a long moment, aware of his shuddering breath, the rapid pulse thudding against his ribs and he pressed his forehead hard into the bark of the tree, sucking in slow, steady gasps of green scented air. His pulse slowed and he listened. The forest had gone still, the smaller creatures were hiding from the fury of the pursuit. Then came the soft sound of leaves crushed, a snuffle of breath. Euan kept his face pressed against the tree, tilting it slowly, so slowly, until the forest floor came into view. The large wolf walked out from the surrounding trees, muzzle bearing fresh stains.

The other, smaller, wolves followed after, teeth glinting in the growing light, tongues lolling as they huffed for breath. The wolf stared up into the oak, straight at Euan's hiding place. It turned its head to the larger of the two wolves that followed it. Its tawny fur glimmered in the light that fell through from above. The wolf shuddered, a shiver running through it from nose to tail. It twitched and pulsed and the wet sounds of flesh reshaping itself filled the quiet. Euan wanted to look away, desperately needed to close his eyes, to not see. Then, quickly, mercifully, it was done. Euan swallowed hard against the bile that coated his throat, eyes fixed on the naked woman that stood proud in the pale glimmer of dawn.

"We know you're up there. Ye might as well come down, I'm no going to be happy if I have to climb up there to get ye." The woman swiped at the blood that coated her chin, tongue running out over her lips before she smiled, the expression all teeth and no merriment. "We've already got the rest of your men; unfortunately you've lost one of them. Broke his neck when he fell; even we can't heal that. But the other three will be fine, once they heal up. Well, as fine as they can be now they're one of us."

Euan dragged his gaze away from her naked figure, the plump swell of breast and hip doing nothing to distract him from her bloodied mouth, the threat in her words. "What..." Euan coughed, swallowed hard and tried again. "What are ye?"

"Now, surely you're not that stupid. Did ye never get fairy stories afore bed?" The woman laughed, sinking her hand deep into the dark ruff of fur on the large wolf's neck. He turned, making a mock snap at her arm and she laughed again, the sound merry and light.

"We're shifters. Weres. The two-natured. And now so are your men. So ye can either come down here nicely and join our little clan, and we'll try and make it as pleasant as we can, considering we're going to have to bite you. Or..." At this point the male wolf growled, a deep and threatening rumble, teeth bared. "I'll have to come up that tree and throw ye down, which is going to make me extremely annoyed, and John here won't be so gentle with ye. Your choice."

Euan had heard the rumours that the king was paying an extra bounty for wolves. He had thought about hunting them for the money it would bring but he had had no idea that maybe the king wasn't as mad as people thought. There was something to his proclamations saying evil stalked the land. He closed his eyes, and hoped that once he opened them, he would find himself curled beneath his plaid, with his men sleeping around him. But the tree felt far too real beneath his cheek, and the scents of greenery and blood were too strong to be imaginary. Eyelashes lifted, and he stared down at the woman. He shook his head, not really believing the situation he was in and moved out from the shadow of the trunk, revealing himself to the group below as he dropped to sit on the branch.

"Why us?" The question was strangely plaintive like a child's plea against the monsters in the dark or like the child's wailing against the uncaring continuation of the universe when everything you thought was true was ripped away.

The woman laughed again, but this time there was no humour at all to the sound, before she once again curled her fingers in to the wolf's, John's, fur. "You've been a busy boy these last couple of days. Brought your group to our attention with your little kidnapping. Could be that that fat lord of yours has something we want. We think he's carrying information. Information that could put us in danger. You will have noticed the bounty on wolves has risen. Why do you think that is? The new king isn't taking too kindly to our existence, thinks we're the devil's work. He's attempting to wipe us out."

The two wolves flanking her growled and their fur bristled. The woman took in a deep breath, her breasts rising and Euan felt himself flush. He had never been in the company of a naked woman for so long and even though he felt no arousal, it was still uncomfortable. She let the breath out, forcing her anger away, smiling softly as the wolf beside her licked at her hand.

She continued, "And we have been watching you. You and your men. You can hunt, remain hidden when needed. You are strong, loyal to your men, as they are to you. John believes, as do I, that you will be a good addition to our Clan. And it wasn't like I could have just walked in there, demanded that you let us search your prisoners, was it? So here we are, and this is the last time I'm asking. Are ye coming down, or am I coming up?"

Euan gave a half grin in an attempt to try to hide his fear as he realised that he had very little choice. It wasn't as if anyone was going to come to his rescue. But, how bad could joining them be? They looked well-fed, the woman curved in all the right places, while the two wolves beside her were packed with muscle.

He thought back to the group he and his fellow hunters had left behind. Their bodies were honed lean and hard by the cold winters, the lack of food and shelter reducing their numbers slowly each year. The woman had mentioned something about the rest of his men earlier, that they were already part of whatever this was in front of him. If this was true, without their hunters the women and children would starve out here in the forest., But then perhaps, without the men, the women would be able to ease their way back into the small villages, or to go home. The children could have houses, the women new husbands. It would be easier for them without Euan and his men to worry the townsfolk.

But strangers were unwelcome in these troubled times. Thoughts ran back and forwards in his mind as he tried to decide on the best course of action. Maybe he could persuade this clan of... wolves... Weres... to take the rest of his people in and take care of them. It was worth a try at least, he couldn't see his way to a better answer.

He shrugged, "Seems like we'll do it your way, m'lady." The woman grinned, sharp and bright, and watched as Euan swung his body down, dropping lightly to the ground. He straightened up and tried to hide his nerves behind a veneer of bravado as he approached the woman.

"Take off your shirt, handsome. Wouldn't want it to get ripped and bloody now would we?" Euan smiled at her, pulling his shirt over his head.

"So where d'ye want me, darling?" Euan forced a grin to his lips as he spoke. She laughed at Euan's bravado. She seemed to find him amusing and Euan flushed a little as the smaller female wolf snorted and bared her teeth in the lupine equivalent of a laugh. Euan blinked then, and the flush faded rapidly as he realised that, in the brief moment his head had been shrouded in the fabric of his shirt, the other wolf had disappeared.

"Oh, I don't want ye anywhere. But I think John is fine with ye right there." She smiled again and Euan whipped round, instinctively backing away. It seemed that was all that was needed to trigger the hunting instinct and Euan tried to freeze but the huge wolf leapt, landing hard against Euan's chest. Euan sprawled backwards, and the bare skin along his spine scraped on the hard soil. But that was suddenly the least of his worries as warm breath, which was scented with the deep copper taste of fresh blood and the cloying rank sweetness of decaying flesh, brushed over his face.

Sudden pain shot through his shoulder, flaring out from two points, then four before turning into just pressure that hurt and, oh God, the pulling and shaking. Euan wanted to scream, but all the air had shot out of his system when he hit the ground and all he could manage was a faint squeak of a gasp. Then as quickly as it came the pressure was gone, the remaining ache throbbed with each pulse of blood, spreading through his body. His lungs jerked against his ribs, and forced him to inhale while it felt like his blood was on fire, tracing through his veins with the burn of too strong whisky. Euan arched on the ground, back bowing almost inhumanly as the scream finally ripped its way free.

When Euan came to, he was huddled around himself, his knees curled up tight to his chest on his side, and there was the slick of something wet and rough brushing repetitively over his shoulder. He laid there with eyes closed, the drum of his heartbeat loud in his ears, with the soft lazy sound of bees providing counterpoint. Birds chirped and fluttered overhead in a random scatter of melody. Memories flooded back in, and he remembered the hunt. *The hunt!* He flipped over on to his back, expecting pain, but his shoulder just ached dully. He realised the wet roughness was a tongue, that a tongue was licking his shoulder. His nose crinkled in disgust, and he sneezed at the sudden burst of scent that assailed him.

Rolling to his knees, he backed away from the wolf that had been standing over him; it was a different one this one, although how he knew the difference he wasn't quite sure. The wolf just huffed out a breath, with its tongue lolling between long white canines, and collapsed belly down in the vacated patch of sunlight.

A low, deep rumble of a laugh rolled across the clearing. Euan blinked and rose to his feet, looking round to see a man standing in a shaft of light. His plaid was wrapped loosely round his hips. He was broad shouldered; he stood with his scarred chest bare in the sunlight and thick hair the same grey-sprinkled black as the wolf that had bit him.

"Welcome to the clan, son!"

Chapter 3
Merging Clans

The clearing in the forest had become busier during Euan's slip into unconsciousness, the old oak shading several new people. Euan took a long moment to convince himself that the morning's events had really occurred, the purple bruising over his shoulder was a damn fine reminder of the truth of it, an unescapable reminder. He sighed and rubbed at it before he turned his thoughts to what the woman had said.

Pushing himself up from the ground, he blinked as he brushed the remains of dried leaves and grasses from his bare skin. The sun had moved higher in the sky, making it nearly noon. The chase must have taken more out of Euan than he realised. He rubbed at his shoulder absently as he asked the dark haired man, "Where are the rest of my men, the hunting party?"

The demand would have been better if his voice hadn't broken in the middle of it; thirst was clawing at his throat, causing him to cough as pain shot through him. The dark haired man gestured and a young blonde girl went running off, with her skirts rising around her calves to expose bare feet, before she returned with a carved wooden cup and a waterskin. The older man took his time filling the cup before he passed it over to Euan.

"My men?" Euan's voice was rough, scratchy, as he wrapped his fingers around the cup but he kept his gaze steady as he waited for an answer to his question.

John sighed and shook his head a little, shooting an exasperated look at Euan before he grinned a little, teeth flashing white against the dark of his beard. He rocked back on his heels and Euan noticed that his legs were also bare beneath his plaid, toes sinking back into the leaf litter as he leaned over to push the cup upwards to Euan's mouth.

"Mostly in the same sorry state as ye are son, apart from one. Ellen mentioned him to ye, this morning? We are sorry. We dinnae like that kind o' thing to happen, but he just fell badly, hitting his head against a fallen trunk, and there was nothing tae be done for him after that. Ye can see them all soon, but drink first."

Euan gulped the chilled liquid greedily, caring little about the droplets that spilled over his chin, running down the bare skin of his chest. He wiped his fingers over his ribs once he had finished, feeling the bones far too prominent beneath his skin. John threw his shirt at him and Euan pulled it over his head before sending a questioning glare at him.

"All right, son, this way then. Might as well tell all of ye together, saves repeating myself anyway. Meg, be a darlin' and go fetch Robert and your mother. Time to make the introductions."

John led the way through the trees, following an almost invisible path until the canopy thinned out overhead and they made their way into another clearing, a smaller stream running along the side of it, willows dipping their slender branches down towards the clear burble.

Euan sent a quick glance round, and found Bran, Niall, and Connor seated on the grass, while some of John's men stood watch around the open space. Euan knew then it was Ruaridh they had lost to the broken neck. Soon there would be another grave under the trees. He'd have to ask John where the body was so they could give the man a proper burial. His men visibly relaxed as he walked across the clearing towards them, and he could see the worry draining from them now there was someone to take charge, to show them the way.

The older woman from the previous night was over by the stream, dressed this time in a long skirt and jacket, her hair half hidden under a scarf. The young girl knelt beside her. She was dressed in a similar fashion but her blonde hair was uncovered.. It was obvious that they were related and Euan felt himself colour slightly as the memory of the flesh hidden under the long dress popped into his mind. Another older man made his way over to them, meeting Euan and John halfway across the space. He was shorter than them both, his beard auburn and grey, hair close cropped and thinning slightly on top. He smiled and clapped John on the arm.

John returned the gesture and said, "Robert! How are the new lads holding up? This is Euan here. Euan, this is Robert, my Fear-Taic or second in command if ye will."

Robert nodded briefly at Euan before turning back to John. "Ach, they're as well as tae be expected after the night they had. Taking a lot o' it on faith. Things'll no doubt go better now we have yer boy here. Come, I think Ellen and Meg are brewing up some tea. Always makes things better I find."

Euan nodded at the other man and followed him across, patting shoulders and clasping arms with his men, taking in the blood-stained shirts and wide, confused stares they shot him at his seeming ease with the strangers.

"It's going tae be fine lads, apparently the explanation is on its way, along with a cup o' tea." He perched himself on a boulder and watched as everyone made their way across. Ellen and Meg brought wooden cups filled from the kettle that hung over the small fire.

Once they were all settled around; John seated on another out-cropping of rock, Bobby to his right, Ellen and Meg to his left and the others arranged in a loose circle; John cleared his throat and began. "This has probably all come as a bit o' a surprise to ye all. Being chased by wolves and then waking up tae us lot."

"Better than being dead at least!" Bran muttered, fingers tugging at his short beard.

"Aye, that it is," laughed John. "Although some of ye may not think so once I've told ye what ye are now. Introductions first though... I'm John, Chief o' this wee Clan here and o' any of the other septs ye might find in this part of our country." He quickly introduced the other Weres.

Meg smiled prettily at her introduction, but it was too sharp, too white, and Euan heard a couple of his men swallow hard. He hoped that none of them tried a quick seduction, it probably wouldn't end well for them. Meg did not seem at all like a simpering village lass.

"To Robert's right is Keir. He'll be your man for most of your questions about the day-to-day running of the pack. Now, I've had the pleasure of meeting Euan early this morning, so why don't the rest of you give us a name?"

Silence fell as no-one wished to speak first. Euan sighed and then quickly introduced his men. "Ruaridh is the one with the broken neck. We'd like his body tae bury if ye dinnae mind."

"Of course, of course. Well, I think the easiest thing to do about this little situation is to show you lads. Keir, would ye mind? Now you'll no be able tae do this yourself until the first full moon. About a year after that and ye should be getting closer to controlling it all..." John continued as Keir rose to his feet and pulled off his shirt, shoes and began to unwrap his plaid. There was a nervous laugh from Niall and a whistle from Meg which Keir returned with a wink. Soon he was standing there naked as the day he came into the world. There was a short moan as Keir dropped to his knees, then a couple of wet crunches, accompanied by cries of surprise from the men to either side of Euan. Then where Keir had been standing was a wolf, coat shot through with the same reddish glints as the man's hair.

There was a scrabbling sound from Euan's left and he turned to see Niall, arse planted in the remains of last year's fallen leaves, eyes wide, mouth working silently as his legs and arms tried to move him away from the gathering.

"Niall. Niall!"

"Witchcraft, Euan. Witchcraft! We're all going to burn. God save me. In nomine Patri..."

Niall managed to make it to his feet, eyes still showing the whites, lips mumbling prayers before he turned and fled into the trees. The wolf turned and looked at John, who nodded briefly, before it turned and gave chase. Euan turned to the two remaining members of his group.

"Bran. Connor. You lads good? Or am I going to have to give ye a wee smack to stop ye fleeing into the trees as well?"

"No, I'm no leaving. If what the man says is true and he can show me how to do that and show us how to hunt so that we can look as well-fed as his lot..." Bran took a sip from his tea and smiled over at Robert and John.

"Connor? You with us too, lad?" Connor, the youngest member of Euan's tiny group, nodded his head, fair hair tumbling into his eyes which he pushed back with an impatient hand, revealing eyes wide with wonder.

"What about the rest of my men, will ye take them, too? There's another couple of men back at our camp guarding the English prisoners we took, and we have our women, some bairns." Euan stared at John, watching his face carefully as John thought for a long moment, before he exchanged swift glances with Robert and Lady Ellen.

"Aye. The men we'll take, if they will join us. The women will get a choice to remain with the pack as humans or to take the bite. If we change them, their chances of bearing any further bairns would be very much less. We wouldnae bite the bairns, their bodies, their minds, are too unformed. It would kill them. But obviously they will remain with their families and they will get offered full pack status once they are grown." John rubbed a hand through his hair and continued after taking a long drink from his cup. "As to the prisoners, they are yours. If you get a ransom for them, we will help you to return them. If not, we will also help you to take them far away from here and let them make their way back to wherever they came from. All we ask is that you let one of us question them to see if they are carrying anything that will cause us problems. And that none of you give them any sign of what we are. Our situation is dangerous enough."

Euan nodded to that condition before he asked, "And what of those who dinnae want what your Clan is offering? Ye've taken our choice away but I think those of us here can live with that. But what of the others?" Euan had to ask, even though he feared the answer.

"We are sorry for that." John did look genuinely pained at the thought. "We don't usually change people without their knowledge, but as you know, times are hard, we are all under pressure from the king and his lords. Your people can either join us, or they can try and survive the next winter, without their hunters, without their menfolk, take their chances with the villages nearby, we'd let you see them safely there. But I can tell ye now lad, and ye probably already ken this – they'll no get a better offer than this one. Every addition to our clan gives us another hunter. They'll be stronger, we'll be stronger together. It's maybe no the best of lives, but in the world we have to live in, don't ye think ye should give them the chance?"

Euan nodded thoughtfully and rose to his feet. "Can I take a spell tae think about it?"

John nodded and Euan met the gazes of his remaining men, noting the acceptance in their eyes. He walked slowly into the trees, starting a slow circle round the camp. Walking had always helped him think. He felt at home in the forest, and his developing senses only made him feel more comfortable, out there amongst the trees, the air quiet around him as he wandered in and out of patches of dappled sunlight.

He thought about their camp. It was well defended, but only against man. They had no defence against hunger, disease or the harsh winters. The prisoners were a drain on their already stretched resources and if they could not get a ransom, their chances of surviving the next winter were slim. Their women had already lost husbands and he knew they could not afford to lose more; he was well aware that John would not suffer a lone wolf around his territory, even if it was one he had made himself.

All of John's men were sturdy looking, bodies lean, but packed with muscle, lacking the starved look some of his men were starting to develop, food passed to the children and the women in their group. He tried to think of any problems they might have with joining the larger Clan. There would be tussling for position no doubt, both with the men and the women. He knew that Maeve was used to being the woman in charge, and she might bridle at suddenly losing her top spot, but it would be the same if they moved back to a village. He had to give them the choice, and he had to show them what he thought was the right choice.

Turning on his heel, Euan moved swiftly back to the clearing and walked towards John who rose slowly to his feet, his head lifting and shoulders widening, the closest his human form could get to the wolf's need to show its dominance. Euan looked quickly towards his men, noting their small nods. They knew his decision had been made. He approached John slowly and held out his hand, clasping it around the thick forearm John held out to him. He held eye contact with the older man as he slowly dropped to one knee.

"I pledge my fealty."

John nodded once and placed his hand on Euan's shoulder. Euan dropped his gaze in a small gesture of submission, but refused to bow his head. A small smile flickered over John's face, before he said solemnly, "Clan Ranulf accepts your pledge. Rise, Euan and be welcome."

Robert and Ellen both welcomed Euan, the others nodding to him in recognition, echoing the welcome. Euan rose to his feet and Connor and Bran came forward and made their own oaths, changing their world forever.

Chapter 4
Running From the Past

Tris stared at the roiling clouds of dark smoke that rose lazily into the blue sky. He had been able to see them for a while now, but had been hoping against hope that things would not be as bad they seemed. He felt his eyes sting as he watched another apple tree topple over in the orchard, flames finally weakening it past its point of survival. The fields were already bare and blackened and he had seen several servants on the road, carts laden with whatever items they had managed to salvage or steal. Their chances were slim and Tris had just joined them, a servant without a master was easy pickings.

Later that day Tris managed to ask one of the fleeing serfs about the whereabouts of Sir Christopher, only to be told that the lord had left the keep almost as soon as he had arrived there, after a messenger from York had come racing into the courtyard, horse lathered and breathing heavy. The servant of course had no idea as to the message the man had carried, only knew that Sir Christopher had packed up that very night, and his carriage had left at first light not two days ago. The soldiers had moved in the following day, stealing and torching everything.

Lord Barnard's instructions had been to return to York if Sir Christopher was not at the keep; the Church also wanted him to return to York, to the Cathedral; but Tristan didn't want to walk himself into a trap. He'd been placed with Lord Barnard by the Church and the duke. The supposition had been that Lord Barnard was not either clever enough or important enough to draw attention to himself, but they had obviously not counted on the gambling habit that had quickly spun out of control and which had left him deep in debt to some rather unsavoury money lenders. They had tried to sweep the problem away by sending the hapless lord north. Out of sight, out of mind they hoped. So now Tristan was left without a place, left to make his own way back to Court or Church, knowing only that if he were to be recognised by the wrong man, he would end up being roasted, perhaps quite literally, to find out the information and secrets he carried.

Tris crept as quietly as he could around the keep, finding part of the kitchen where a heavy beam had held most of the roof up and he curled up for a little while, knowing that he would be able to think better if he was not so tired. The following morning he hacked his hair off with his knife, leaving the nape of his neck feeling uncomfortably tender and exposed. The rough cut lowered his status instantly and he scrabbled through the rubble, finding a leather jerkin and an undyed linen shirt that had obviously belonged to one of the men who had worked in the keep. He thought about looking for a new position, somewhere in the countryside, but discarded the idea quickly. The other displaced serfs and slaves had a head start and no-one would even look twice at him when it came to farm work, his hands bore no calluses and he had no working knowledge of how to run a plough or heft a scythe.

Over the next few weeks, Tris moved south and east, down towards the bigger towns and cities, seeking gossip and information. After much loitering in shadowy corners of taverns and inns he discovered that Lord Barnard had not made ransom.

"He's lucky he's not in the debtors gaol," his source whispered over the third pot of ale Tris had bought for him. "Better dead than that. Think he went back to his mother's home, somewhere out in the country. Heard there were other people looking for him too, something about a message or a companion."

A grubby hand slid across the table, palm upwards. "Cross it with silver and there might be more information in a couple of days." The man winked at him, his smile exposing rotting teeth. Tris shuddered and shook his head.

"No, that will not be necessary. 'Twas just idle curiosity, no more. My mistress does like a good bit of gossip now and then." Tris thought it better to pretend he had somewhere to go just in case there were other rumours going around about a missing companion. It was definitely not the time to be seen as a lone wanderer.

Tris thought about making his way back to the Church, but, as he had travelled south, some of the things he had heard had him doubting his faith. Priests were exhorting their flocks to be aware of sinners, of witches, to turn against their fellow men and report them for their sins. No one had yet forgotten the hanging of eight women and two men in Lancaster, all accused of consorting with the devil. Tris just hoped that this wasn't a sign of things to come, that maybe it was just a few over-zealous churchmen. He had no lord anymore, but he still had the Church.

Then, in one small village just north of York, Tristan finally saw the troubles with his own eyes. He watched aghast but unable to leave or interfere as a young woman was bound to a chair, accused of various forms of witchcraft and consorting with the Devil himself. Tris wanted to cry out, to say that there was no proof, that she was just a young girl, but as a stranger he was more than likely to end up beside her. He watched, tears welling in his eyes as they pushed her into the river in a bid to rid her of her demonic possession, saying that the lord would save her if she was as innocent as she claimed.

The last image Tris had of her was her wide blue eyes and pale hair, sinking below the water. He felt part of his faith drown with her. How could his God allow this to happen? He spent that night curled up in a small ball, hidden amongst last year's hay at the back of a barn on the outskirts of the village. How was Tristan to explain his escape not only from the Scots but also from the downfall that now tainted his former lord? There would be some only too happy to accuse him in a bid to permanently bury the secrets he carried.

Instead, he kept away from the cities and the Church, kept moving south. He managed to pick up the occasional job, getting nothing more than food and sometimes, if he was particularly lucky, a roof over his head. As his body grew, he'd found more work; just now he had a regular job as a farrier's assistant, his soft voice and strong figure calming and holding the horses steady whilst they were being shod. The work was adding bulk to his height, his biceps and thighs thickening, catching up with his broadening shoulders.

After almost nine months of travelling he had stopped here and was, at least temporarily, settled in a small room above the stables. After a month of stability and safety he allowed his curiosity to get the better of him and he opened the small satchel that had been with him since his escape. He remembered the small case the Bishop had pressed into his hand, a thin crimson braid spiralling around the narrow cylinder, the heavy wax sealing the ends. It should have been handed to a cleric that would have met him at Lord Barnard's keep. He also had the papers his lord had passed to him that morning in the forest and he opened those first.

By the flickering light of a tiny stub of candle he quickly read each missive, eyes wide. Perhaps this could be his way out, a new beginning for him. This could be his chance to perhaps rebuild the family that had been taken from him by the Church, somewhere safe and far away. He had no idea whether his parents still lived, if his little sister had made a good match. He had been promised that they would receive the Church's grace, but he had seen recently how untrustworthy the Church was. He was sure that his skills as both a farrier and someone who could both read and write would assure him passage on the ship mentioned in the missives. The fact that the ship was to leave from Scotland was of no hardship, perhaps even of benefit. His fingers wavered over the separate case that had been passed to him by the Bishop, but something stayed his hand. Perhaps the Church's hold was still too strong yet for him to break the ties completely. It felt not just like a betrayal of trust, but of faith as well. Or perhaps it just wasn't time for it to be opened. He shook his head at himself.

Even though he knew now that he bore very little resemblance to the slight, long-haired page boy that he had been, Tris had been avoiding moving back northwards. But now, with this news, he could leave the country for a new life and he was sure that he could avoid the city of York on his way back to Scotland.

He decided to leave that night. The next morning he took some of the money he had carefully built up, bought himself boots more suited to travelling, a warmer cloak and some other essentials and said his goodbyes to the farrier and his family. Out of habit he found himself heading back towards Lord Barnard's lands. It was where he had been brought up, he knew the area well and, despite everything, he had felt safest there.

From there he followed the path they had taken on his first, ill-fated, journey into Scotland. Tris continued on and passed through what should have been Lord Barnard's new lands. The fields were overrun with wild grasses, dandelions and clover offering their bobbing heads to the heavy drone of bees and the buzz of the small black flies that filled the air at this time of year. Nature had moved into the keep as well, grasses springing up in the cracks of the flagged stone floor, the stable roof already half collapsed, birds flying in and out of the arrow slits that broke up the tower walls. A few brave souls had moved back, taking advantage of the ready cut pieces of stone, the cleared land.

He had also run into a small group of soldiers, and he had moved into the undergrowth at the side of the narrow road as they marched past. Their commander had reined in his horse, a large chestnut gelding, and stared down at Tris curiously.

"Why are you out here on your own, lad? Not a deserter, are we?"

Tris kept his head lowered, slouched his shoulders and bent his knees slightly, trying to look smaller and less worthy of notice.

"No, Sir," he mumbled. "On an errand for my master, Sir. Went to check out a horse on the farm yonder. See if it needed shoeing, Sir. Your horse could probably do with a new one on its off fore, I can see it's come a bit loose, Sir." Tris kept adding the honorifics, letting his accent slip into the more local style.

"Ah, farrier's lad are we boy? Well, carry on then. But be careful lad. Wolves in the woods here and Scots. Murderous bastards, the whole lot of them. Don't let us find you wandering round like this again lad. Terrible things could happen to a young man out here. Tell your master that we could be dropping by."

Tris nodded and raised his hand to his forehead, keeping his gaze lowered as the small group moved off. The warnings had been less than subtle and Tris decided he needed to get off the road, at least for a little while.

Now, sitting in a lonely Inn, one of the way posts on the way north, Tris wondered briefly why no-one else had taken over the keep. The lands were fertile enough, there were several springs nearby that ran down from the rising hills to the North, bringing clear, fresh water. Maybe it was just too far from the king, from London, or the fact that it was situated in the Scottish lowlands, the area prone to attack by reivers. Or perhaps the common folk associated the taint that had brought the lord down with the land itself. No doubt King James would soon enough assign the land to some new lackey eager to seek favour and perhaps what money could be eked from the land and its inhabitants.

Tris sat slouched in his chair, trying to disguise his height. Although he was pleased that he had grown, it made it much harder from him to melt into shadows or to disappear into a crowd and it was also beginning to intimidate other men, as they wondered whether he intended to be a rival for their position or their women. He stared moodily down into the dark depths of the ale in front of him, a maudlin feeling creeping over him. Perhaps the ale was to blame as he pondered his reasons for this last journey towards the vast unknown.

He thought about blaming his troubles on that Scottish rogue that had captured them, but truth be told, things had been changing long before then. Alliances shifted quicker than clouds in these troubled times and Tris was sure that sooner or later he would have been pulled from his former master and only God could say whether his position then would have been better than where he was now.

But life went on, and thankfully, even here on this lesser used road, people still wanted a drink, travellers and merchants still needed somewhere to stay for the night. In fact Tris was surprised at how busy it was when he decided to spend some of his all too quickly dwindling supply of coins on a roof over his head and a hot meal. The thick stew had been tasty enough, settling warm and comforting in his stomach. The serving girl had giggled at him and brought him a second bowl, placing her finger to her lips with a slight shake of her head when he reached for his coin.

Tris returned her smile with one of his own, but kept it small and vague enough not to give her any further ideas. He had realised early in life that his tastes did not run to those of the fairer sex and his affiliations to the Church and to his lord had left him little time for dalliances. He had managed to avoid any compromising situations with protestations of piety. However, it was a lonely life he was being forced to lead and he felt the urge to settle down, to make some sort of family, more and more strongly.

The king's recent mood swings and changes of opinion seemed to be threatening that chance more and more. Up until recently, although it had not been encouraged, it had been acceptable for second or third sons to enjoy dalliances or even longer relationships with a male friend. But now, with the king's new show of piety, came stricter rules, the Church elders seeming all too happy to find yet more ways of restricting people's lives or of threatening them into compliance. Tris thoughts turned to the Northampton witch trials, where several people had been dunked, one of them a man. The rumours had it that he had been found guilty of letting the devil sodomise him. And now people said that the act was something the devil drove you to, something unnatural, unsanctioned by the good lord.

Tris pulled away from his maudlin, somewhat fearful thoughts and felt thankful instead for the fact that he had also managed to get a room, tucked up under the eaves. Well, not so much a room as a walled off space, barely large enough for the pallet that lay on the floor, but it was shelter from the night life. The ale was a welcome addition, the bitter, hoppy taste sliding all too easily down, adding to the warm, pleasantly full feeling. He tipped his head back, allowing the last mouthful to slide down the back of his throat, before he moved, pushing himself up from the table and heading for his room.

Lying on the uncomfortable pallet, Tris tossed and turned, unable to find sleep. The faint noises of other guests travelled up through the floor along with the occasional stamp of hooves from the stable yard outside. He found his mind floating back again, perhaps influenced by his location and his earlier thoughts. The image of Euan appeared behind his eyes; tawny sun-kissed hair, the firm muscles of his calves, the broad shoulders.

Tris found himself trying to imagine what lay under the loose linen shirt, the length of fabric that wound round those slender hips. He moaned quietly as he felt himself stiffen, sliding a hand down under the scratchy woollen blanket. He pressed his hand against his cock, knowing that he should not indulge, not here in this busy inn. The

Euan in his head parted his lips slightly, hands going to the buckle that held his plaid up and Tris gave in to the vision.

Loosening his breeches, he wrapped a hand around himself, pushing the blankets away with the other. He ran his fingers up and down his shaft, just brushing the skin lightly, a tease. He let his feet push against the floor as his hips rose slightly, pushing into his hand. He trailed both hands up over the flat plain of his stomach, scraping his nails over nipples that had already pebbled in the cool air, biting his lip to swallow the small sound he made.

One hand continued up to his mouth, where he licked at the palm, leaving it sticky wet with saliva. He wrapped that hand around himself again, the movement easier this time with the thin layer of lubrication. The imaginary Euan had now dropped to his knees in front of Tris, and Tris shoved the side of his arm into his mouth as his hand began to slide faster, grip tightening as desire spiralled higher inside him.

He brought his hand back to his mouth, could smell the musky scent of himself on his palm as he licked at it again. Both hands lowered this time, one cupping his balls, rolling the small orbs under their velvet coat of skin as the other grasped his cock firmly, sliding rapidly up and down his length. He wished he could see, could watch the fat pink head grow slick, but instead he thought about brushing it over the line of Euan's cheekbone, the curve of his mouth. He imagined a tongue, slipping just a little way between those plush lips, just the faintest touch on the heated skin of his shaft.

His hand tightened and his body jerked, teeth clenching as he tried to remain silent as his seed spilled out of him, sticky warm across the taut skin of his belly. Breath gusted out of him on a quiet sigh and he rose to his feet on slightly shaky legs. Holding his breeches with one hand he made his way to the small basin and ewer that sat on a shelf just below the small window that let the soft glow from the moon fill the room. He stared absently out towards the trees as he rinsed the sticky residue from his stomach. It took him a long moment for his brain to realise what the movement along the tree line was. A small curse slipped free as all thoughts of sleep fled and he turned to once more collect his belongings and leave.

Chapter 5

Through the Forest

Euan frowned, slapping softly at his arm as another enterprising insect tried to make a late night snack out of him. He stared hard at the inn, watching as lights slowly went out in the windows. His men had been watching the inn for a while, the steady flow of customers, despite the rural locale, attracting their attention. Either the innkeeper offered very good ale or this was a meeting point for the transfer of goods and information. Euan was definitely hoping for the latter, although, as he slapped away another insect, he wouldn't say no to a nice pause inside and a cool drink of ale away from these damnable insects.

The inn seemed nearly full, horses filled every stall in the stables, and spilled out to the nearby field, tethered to the ground with stakes. Several coaches were also resting in the field, guards lying slumped against them, heads nodding, hands slapping at the biting wildlife. Euan worked his way back towards his men, taking one last chance to run over their plan. Although his wolf was good for many things, the nuances of planning were beyond him in that form.

The moon hid her rounded fullness behind veils of cloud, playing peek-a-boo with the world below. Her pale light caught the silver highlights in the brindled fur of the two wolves that were slinking slowly out from the tree-line. They crept, bellies low, in a long circle, moving downwind of the field that held the now dozing horses. Euan noticed the two wolves creeping slowly closer and gave the signal to his men, sending them quietly down the hill towards the inn.

Euan gave a soft hoot and the wolves rose, stiff-legged, fur bristling. White teeth glinted razor sharp before muscles bunched in their haunches and they sprang over the makeshift fence, teeth nipping at flanks and hocks. Euan kept watching as the two wolves dodged in and out of the flailing hooves, snapping tethers and knocking stakes loose. As soon as each horse felt its restraint loosen, it followed basic animal instinct, fleeing the immediate darkness of tooth and claw for the dubious safety of the surrounding hills. Euan knew that the guards in the neighbouring field were already unconscious, bodies hidden beneath the sheltering bulk of the carts they had failed to guard.

As he approached the inn, candlelight flared from within, and he could hear footsteps pounding against the wooden floors. Figures spilled from the door only to be met with the kiss of cold steel against the tender flesh of throat or stomach. He could scent the panic spreading quickly through the inn as others cried out, but the inhabitants found all the exits blocked and soon his men had every occupant kneeling on the hard packed earth in the courtyard in front of the inn, hands bound roughly behind their backs. Those that had put up more of a fight also sported an assortment of rapidly swelling bruises and oozing cuts.

Euan blinked, nose twitching at the heavy smell of blood and fear that made its way through the scarf that hid his face. He stared along the line of prisoners and smiled, grin full of dark promise, as he surveyed his handiwork. It was good that they were afraid of him, afraid of his men. Maybe it would keep some of them away in the future, stop the almost constant encroachments into land that did not belong to them. He could hear the kitchen maids sniffling, trying to stifle tears, but he had no time to mollycoddle his captives.

"You gentlemen make yerselves comfortable. I'll no keep ye long." He turned to the slim man behind him. "Well then, shall we go search, see what we can find? Mebbe some of these lovely gentlemen will have brought us a gift." He could see Lachlan's eyes crinkle, knew there was a hungry smile hidden behind the scarf that concealed their identities.

Euan felt somewhat uncomfortable. He had survived for long enough without robbing random travellers or actually killing anyone. The kidnap and ransom attempt had been carefully planned on the information they had had. There had only been one fatality, the guard killed by Bran's arrow. They had no reason to know that it would go so wrong once the demand was made. The winter had been harsh and many lands were no longer safe for man or wolf to hunt on. Game-keepers were more common, the new Lairds employing men strictly to protect deer and grouse. Also, word had come to them that the pack's secret had been discovered and information was being passed to the king's men in Scotland, with explicit details of their encampments.

The task had been given to Euan to find out if this rumour was true, so Euan and Lachlan moved carefully upstairs. Euan's knife glinted in the candlelight, while his sword was tucked safely down the length of his spine. They swiftly but steadily worked their way through each room, stacking saddlebags and chests out in the narrow hallway. As Euan entered the last, tiny, room, he paused. Eyelashes flickered down over dark eyes as he inhaled. The small room reeked of sex to his sensitive nose, but only of one person. A small grin curved his lips for a moment as he pictured the act. The scent of the stranger permeated the room, and there was something so familiar about it, something from his past. He frowned though as he realised that the scent did not belong to any of their prisoners outside. It suggested unfinished business.

Someone had been in this room. Someone that wasn't downstairs. Green eyes shot open and he quickly scanned the room, finding nothing but that fading, almost familiar scent, and the faint warmth lingering in the thin sheet that covered the makeshift pallet.

He grabbed Lachlan and hauled him close, whispering urgently in his ear.

"We have a runner. I'm leaving ye in charge in here, ye know what we're looking for. I want every piece of paper read, every box and bag emptied. Take anything valuable, Ellen and Meg will thank us sure enough for trinkets and coins to be melted down. Search the prisoners as well, then turn them out if ye can. Make sure that none o' them can identify us or where we came from. I want it to seem just like any other raid."

Lachlan nodded grimly, well aware of their precarious existence, and knew anyone who could identify them by name to the Church or the king's men was a threat. He grasped Euan's shoulder briefly. "And we'll meet ye back at the Falls?"

Euan gave a nod in return, giving permission for his troop to head homewards after this search was finished. "Aye, if ye can round up some o' the horses take a cart and some o' the ale casks too, I'm sure the innkeeper will be more than generous to ensure that we're on our way." Euan grinned as he stepped away, a quick, cold show of teeth as he turned to the window at the end of the hall, leaping out and landing in a smooth crouch. The scent was still strong enough for him to pick it up unchanged and he headed off towards the trees in an easy lope.

Tris darted through the trees, sighing at the fact that once more he seemed to be on the run. Every time he thought his life had become more settled and he could relax, since he'd been taken hostage and escaped, he ended up having to run again. Whether it had been a young girl suspicious of why he would not return her attentions, or the Church making people worry about strangers, he never seemed to find anywhere to belong. After seeing one girl drowned and hearing about others bound to stakes and burned alive, he had no hope of sanctuary with the Church. He doubted that he could stand before a priest and meet their eyes without his thoughts showing. This ship was his last hope and he didn't want to miss it.

He kept moving slow enough to avoid making a lot of noise or leaving much of a trail of broken tree limbs and disturbed undergrowth. Thankfully the forests here seemed to be well used by deer and there were plenty of small trails winding amongst the pale trunks of birch, the darker ones of beech and sycamore. Tris knew he couldn't run far in the dark and it made more sense to move at a slower speed and leave less disruption. He could hear the faint sound of rushing water and he angled his path towards the small stream. Although many would have called it cowardly, the way he abandoned the rest of the customers to the bandits, Tris knew he would have made little difference to the outcome. They had been caught by surprise by a well-planned attack. Tris had no sword, no weapon to defend himself. And he knew no-one in the inn, owed loyalty to none, so he had slipped out the window, dropping gently to the ground, and headed swiftly for the cover of the trees. Now he struggled through the darkness beneath the trees, little light making its way through the sheltering branches. A faint brightness came from up ahead and he moved towards it.

Tris found the small stream. The water rushed quick and cold over the pebbled stream bed and he paused to remove his boots and the heavy wool socks beneath, listening carefully for any sounds of pursuit. He had heard the howls of dogs as he had fled, although they sounded odd, more like wolves than hounds. If anyone was to mention his being at the inn, it was possible that they might chase him down, to find out why he had fled, or even just for sport. He wondered if his isolation was making him doubt everyone around him, if it was perhaps making him mad. He had thought it would be freeing to have no allegiances, but instead it was scary; loneliness and paranoia at the motives of those around him had eaten at his soul.

The forest was silent around him, small creatures still and hidden, no sound except the thud of his own pulse and the soft shudders of his breath. Pushing his breeches as far up his muscular legs as they would go, Tris waded into the stream. He sucked in a harsh breath, the water still holding the chill of snow melt from the hills that rose in swelling mounds to the north. The bank on the other side was much steeper and Tris had to wade much further than he would have wished before he was able to scramble up and out the other side.

His teeth chattered from the chill that had spread up from his feet and calves. His skin was white and swollen from the icy water. As Tris moved away from the bank, his feet slid in the long grass that lined the edge of the stream when he headed for the shelter of a large boulder. Pins and needles spread through his lower legs, making him hobble and hop awkwardly, and he accidently sliced his bare foot on an unseen piece of flint. He cursed quietly at the dull pain, knowing that it would sting more once the feeling returned to his cold feet.

Finally, he made it behind the boulder, hidden from the other side of the stream and from anyone who may have seen him running from the inn. Tris rubbed at his feet, forcing the blood back in, the skin reddening and itching. Once his feet began to feel more like his own, he eased his socks and boots back on, knowing that there was not much he could do for the cut at the time. He pulled a chunk of bread from his pack, breaking a small lump off and chewing slowly as he headed off in to the forest. The area felt familiar even in the dark, and Tris was sure that shortly he would come to a cart track that wound through the forest.

The trees started to thin in front of him, one long trunk lying slanted back into the embrace of its brethren, roots pointed dark and dead towards the pale glow of stars. Tris leant a tanned hand against the trunk, wondering if he was far enough from the inn to pause and hide until sunrise. Even though the attack on the inn had nothing to do with Tris and whoever was attacking the inn probably would have no idea who he was, he did not want to end up murdered due to a heritage he had no control over. Tris only wanted to make it on board the ship. He no longer felt part of the Church and held his own faith that his actions would see him through if he kept to what he felt was right.

He tucked himself under the trunk of the tree, the pine needles fragrant beneath his head as he pulled his cloak around his body. Just an hour or so and he would wake again and continue his journey west.

Euan followed the scent into the trees, realising that his prey was more aware, cannier, than he had expected. The trail was easy to follow for Euan, with his sensitive sense of smell, but without that he would have lost the man quickly. He seemed to have moved swiftly but surely through the trees, following the trails left by deer and other wildlife.

Euan groaned as the sound of running water grew stronger. This hunt was suddenly going to get a whole lot harder. It was a matter of honour now. Giving up was not an option for him. The wolf inside bared its teeth in a smile at the challenge. Euan reached the water, crouching to slip a hand in, feeling the chill melt water run through his fingers. He cast about both up and down stream but he knew that his prey has crossed the water, probably wading through it for a while before moving up the far bank. It's what he would have done.

Euan smiled, eyes crinkling at the corners. Finally, someone would make him work for his prize. He moved back towards a willow that curved graceful branches down towards the water, removing his sword then the knives he had hidden in various places. His shoes and hose were next to come off, then his belt. The long length of heavy wool that served as kilt and cloak dropped to pool thickly on the ground. Clad only in his pale linen shirt, Euan wrapped his weapons and footwear in a length of the kilt, before he stripped off his shirt, the night air sending goosebumps trailing over his pale skin. He added the shirt to the bundle and tucked it carefully under the tree.

He moved back towards the river, comfortable in his nakedness. Stretching his arms high, he loosened his muscles, letting his head loll from side to side. He sucked in a deep breath; processing the small, pungent scents of wildlife, the clear aroma of the water, and still, over all those, the faint scent of his prey. Muscles flexed then shifted, rippling his flesh. Bones popped and crunched wetly beneath his skin. The taste of blood filled Euan's mouth as teeth lengthened and his jaw reshaped itself. The soft moan that he could never quite bite back turned into a low growl.

He shook out his new body, fur ruffling before falling flat against his skin. Gold eyes blinked as the wolf adjusted to the sudden change in height, the sounds of the forest much louder to his more sensitive hearing, time and the world dancing around him in a swirl of scent trails. He stretched out his spine again, long front legs sliding out in front, his head lowering, tail twitching. Teeth caught the moonlight, bared by a lupine grin, before Euan tipped his head back and howled softly. The hunt was on.

Euan moved back from the river, looping round, his legs stretching as he built up speed. He hit the riverbank moving fast, pushing hard off the bank, his strong back legs sending him leaping out over the river, splashing into the freezing water more than half way over. He swam strongly, scrambling gracelessly up the far bank, shaking the chill water from his fur in a shower of tiny falling stars. He let the wolf guide him upstream, where the bank rose higher. Then faint, but true, the scent of prey. Euan followed the scent, sneezing as it became stronger. There it was, flattened grass where his prey had climbed up the banking, the dark scent of blood smeared across a sharp stone, a concentration of aromas where the man had paused against a rock, the mixed scents of wool, bread and human.

Euan blinked as he realised his wolf body was rubbing up against the rock, smearing the human's scent, rubbing it into his fur. He snorted, licking at one paw in a distracted fashion before he decided to head back for his clothing then follow the man on two feet. It was slower going as a human and Euan found the crossing the river for the second time much harder, but he did not want to come up against his prey naked and unarmed.

The moon had finally slid below the soft curve of the Earth. The first pale glimmers of dawn glowing softly in the East as Euan drew close to the man he had been tracking. He crept, slow and silent, through the trees, pausing behind a broad trunk. There he was. The man was curled in the hollow beneath a half fallen trunk, with his cloak wrapped around his body, and his head hidden in the shadows. Euan stalked forward, and was drawn by the warm smell, along with the slow pulse of blood. Slowly and carefully he withdrew one of his blades. The dirk was just around the length of his forearm, the blade double-edged and narrowing to a wicked point. He wrapped his fingers around the wood of the grip, worn smooth and moulded to his hand.

Euan remained steady as the man awoke. The man's body went instantly still as he registered the press of steel against the tender skin of his throat. His eyes jerked open and Euan watched his gaze find him, knowing that all his captive would see was the broad sweep of Euan's shoulders against the soft glow of the dawn sky. Euan stifled a smile as he watched the other man try to raise his hands as much as he could even as he was trapped beneath the tree and Euan's blade.

Euan backed up slowly, allowing his captive to slide his body from under the tree. Euan kept the sharp steel blade pressed against the stranger's throat, dissuading him from any thoughts of escape. He blinked as the man slipped his legs out, and couldn't stop his gaze from running down the long, lean muscles shown off by the breeches that clung lovingly to his shape. Euan realised, that once they were standing, the man would be taller than he was.

The young man kept moving slowly across the ground, shifting around as well as sideways. It was what Euan expected him to do, moving so that the growing brightness was no longer at Euan's back. Euan let the point of his knife bite deeper, on the very edge of drawing blood and his prisoner shuffled back, his spine colliding with the fallen trunk. His breath huffed out then stopped altogether when he finally met Euan's cool stare.

The sudden burst of scents from the other man made Euan want to sneeze and he fought the urge to rub at his nose. The bright spike of shock overrode the bitter smell of fear which had flooded out first, followed by a confusion of pheromones. Emotions swept across the man's face, his almond shaped eyes widening in awareness, before dropping closed as something else flickered, too swiftly for Euan to identify it. Then a soft flush coloured the young man's cheeks, the overriding feeling becoming that of anger.

Something niggled at the back of Euan's mind, his wolf growling for attention. He could see the other man staring in confusion as Euan turned away from him, his head tilting to one side, listening to something only he could hear.

"Quick, on yer feet. Now!" The press of steel backed up Euan's urgent whisper and the young man struggled upright, Euan stepping back slightly to allow him to move.

"Move. In front, quick as ye can. Dinnae think of running though; if I don't catch ye, the soldiers coming down the road surely will."

Euan watched as hazel eyes flickered back towards the road, then the taller man's eyes widened in surprise as he finally picked up the faintest sounds of marching feet, the jingle of harness.

"May I take my belongings?" he waved a hand at the bag he had been using as a pillow, the leather soft and worn with age.

"Aye, leave no trace. Now, walk." The point of Euan's dagger jabbed into his captive's back and he moved forward, back into the trees, as indicated.

Chapter 6

Discoveries

After Tris's rather rude and frightening awakening, and his surprising recognition of his captor, the two men had been moving swiftly through the forest for nearly an hour, with Euan shoving Tris left or right to change direction as he required. Ever since he had awoken at the point of Euan's knife, it seemed like the older man had done nothing but order Tris around. Finally, Tris's body began to rebel against the forced march, his mouth was dry and other needs that usually presented themselves in the morning were beginning to make themselves felt more urgently, so Tris just stopped, ignoring the sudden jab at the side of his spine, before spinning round to face his captor.

"So look, I don't know about you, but I cannot keep up this pace without food or water or... other things." Tris made a vague gesture before blushing and continuing. "If you want me to get to wherever we're going, you're going to need to let me stop and have a drink." Tris could hear his voice rising in anger and he almost held his breath, waiting for Euan's response.

"Aye, you're right. Over there." Euan indicated a rocky outcropping, pushing Tris towards it and following behind. "Sit, and take your boots off." Tris blinked, his mouth opening and closing silently.

"Your boots. Off. Are ye simple, man?" Euan's tone was mocking and the corner of his mouth curled in a derisory smirk.

"No!" Tris huffed indignantly. "Just...confused."

"I've no got water with me. I'm going to have to go fetch some and I'd rather have you still here when I get back, so I figure, I take your boots and you don't go for a walk."

Euan smirked, indicating the sharp pieces of splintered rock that littered the ground and the brambles and nettles that twined and twisted in the beams of sunlight that fell through the canopy of leaves above. "Now, ye can either take them off yourself, or I will, but either way...."

Tris sighed then slid his boots off, rolling down his socks too and stuffing them inside. He leant forward, balance somewhat precarious on his rocky perch, to pass his boots to Euan. Euan laughed, his green eyes sparkling in the soft sunshine. "Now, don't you be going anywhere. You don't want me to hunt you down again, trust me." He bared his teeth in what Tris supposed was meant to be a smile, although it looked more like a threat, before he headed off, Tris's boots tucked under his arm.

It didn't take long for Euan to return with a filled waterskin and Tris gulped at the cool liquid greedily, throat working in long swallows. He stared at his captor, with thoughtful hazel eyes, before he finally broke the silence that lay almost comfortably between them.

"So do I get my boots back now? And do you have a name?"

"Aye, here ye go." The boots were tossed carelessly at Tris, who deftly pulled them back on, before sliding down from his rocky perch. He raised an enquiring eyebrow at Euan, waiting to see if the man would answer the other question he had posed. Euan shook his head slightly and smiled somewhat mockingly. "And why would ye be needing a name? So you can sell me out to whichever lord is currently claiming this land belongs tae him?"

"So you were intending on letting me go, then?" Tris's eyebrows raised in surprise as he continued. "And no, I have no idea who is currently claiming ownership of the lands round these parts. I'm just... passing through. I'm Tris." Tris figured that giving away his first name wouldn't hurt, and anyway he already knew Euan's name, even if Euan didn't know that he knew. It might encourage his captor to let him go unhurt.

"Just passing through? That's a dangerous thing tae be doing in these times. The woods are full of murderous Scots, have ye no heard? And the king's soldiers, hunting down poachers and lawless Catholics."

Tris smirked slightly at Euan's echo of the soldier's warning from a couple of days ago before he shrugged and tried to casually look around, hoping to make his movements look aimless as he moved back past Euan towards the tree line. "Well, I've managed to avoid the soldiers so far, and the press gangs..."

Tris let his voice trail off. Euan seemed to be distracted with taking his own drink and Tris started to pivot on one foot. He didn't even manage a full step before a hand clamped around his wrist, grinding the bones together, jerking Tris backwards until he was pressed against Euan's body. His spine arched as Euan curled his other hand around his throat, the waterskin falling to the ground, unnoticed.

"Now, Tris, what kind of behaviour is that? And after I went to all that trouble to get ye a drink, you're just going to run off?" Tris could feel Euan shake his head in mock dismay, felt the hot puffs of air that strangely brought goosebumps to the skin of his neck and shoulders as Euan spoke.

"I was just..."

"Ah-ah, dinnae lie to me Tris. I can tell when you're lying. Now, I think it's time we got ourselves somewhere safe so that we can have a little heart-to-heart about exactly who you are and what you are doing in these parts."

Euan uncurled his fingers from around Tris's neck, and was unable to resist trailing a digit over the rapid pulse at the base of Tris's throat. Tris pulled away jerkily and Euan realised he still had his other hand wrapped tightly round Tris's wrist. He stared at the errant hand for a moment before the fingers loosened their grip. He wondered at the spike of vicious happiness that flooded through him as he noticed the darkening circle of bruises that embraced Tris's wrist.

It was a long trek through the woods. Euan wasn't careless enough to lead anyone directly to any of his clan's safe locations, even if Tris did have the softest looking hair he'd ever seen, and eyes that changed colour like the forest changes colour in the sun. He could sense Tris reaching his limit once more, breath beginning to hitch in his lungs, his once steady gait becoming more of a stuttering limp. He finally heard Tris stumble to a halt, and turned, hiding his smile, pretending to rub at the reddish scruff that chased the line of his jaw.

Tris' head drooped forward, body following, his hands resting on the tops of his thighs, holding himself up. He sucked in a breath and murmured softly, "I can't... Euan, I just can't walk any more. It feels like we have been going in circles and loops and I don't care if you kill me, just let me stop walking." Euan remained still, waiting until Tris realised that he had just called Euan by name, without Euan having introduced himself. And there it was. Head shooting up, Tris paled as the flush of activity drained from his cheeks. Euan watched his mouth open and close, pale lips revealing a flash of pink tongue. Euan could no longer hold it back and he finally gave in to the smirk, letting it crinkle the corners of his eyes.

Tris stared as Euan smiled and then laughed, head tipping back. This was the absolute last thing he had expected. He gaped at Euan, still stunned into silent immobility as the older man strode over, clapping a broad hand against his shoulder. "Ah lad. One day you'll learn tae never underestimate me. And stop yer moaning, we're here."

They passed through a screen of shrubs, living hazel and willow woven together to hide the small shelter constructed in the clearing behind. The single room was basic, a firepit against one wall, a sleeping pallet against the far wall, almost delicate looking shelves holding an assortment of cups and bowls, a cooking pot and a kettle. A table, carved with the same delicacy as the shelves sat with two chairs in the centre of the room, and Tris slumped gratefully into one of them.

Euan laughed again. "Well, make yourself at home then, lad."

"My name is Tris." Tris's indignant reply was somewhat ruined by the groan of relief he made as he slid his boots off and wiggled toes aching from the long trek. He sighed as he realised that one sock was stained rust brown with blood and he tried to recall when it had happened. Then he remembered cutting his foot early that morning. He knew he needed to remove the sock, and it was going to hurt. He turned to ask Euan if there was the possibility of getting some water to heat over the fire that Euan had just started. He blinked, surprised, when he noticed Euan pressed up against the door, as far from Tris as he could get in the small space, eyes wide, lips parted and glistening.

"I...I'll get...water, aye water. That's where I'm going." Euan flew out of the room, returning a few moments later with the filled kettle before disappearing again just as quickly. Tris cleaned himself up, washing face and hands then bathing his sore feet. It was completely dark by the time Euan returned, a small lamp providing the only light apart from the warm glow of the fire.

Euan had brought in two fish which he started to cook. The smell filled the small room, both men nearly ravenous with hunger. Tris split the rest of his bread between them and they devoured the meal in silence. Even though the room was silent and dim, Tris could tell that whatever had spooked Euan earlier had been dealt with, because the older man seemed more relaxed. He thought about what could have made Euan run from the room, but unless he feared the sight of blood, or feet – a small smile curved his mouth at the thought – Tris had no idea.

"Tis too dark now to read. I'll check your bag in the morning. But for now, we'll rest. It's another long walk tomorrow for us." Euan pushed up from the table, stacking the small wooden platters by the door and indicated that Tris should take the far side of the pallet.

"Wouldnae want you to think about running about in the dark, all kinds of terrible things could happen to a man out there at night." Euan gave Tris one of his small grins again. Tris shrugged, and decided he was too tired to care. He dropped boneless to the floor, and crawled across the bedding towards the wall, curling himself under the woollen blanket. He fell into sleep almost immediately, barely noticing as Euan dropped down behind him.

Euan awoke to one of the most tempting smells in the world. He sighed in pleasure, pulling in another deep breath. Hair tickled his nose as he inhaled, and his arm tightened around the warm body curved in front of him as he buried nose and mouth against the nape of a neck, mouthing the hard knob of bone, the heated skin. His eyes flew open as the body jerked out of his arms, a large hand landing flat on his stomach, pushing the breath out of him in an audible rush, as Tris practically vaulted over him to land on his feet halfway across the room.

Grinning, unashamed, Euan stretched languidly before he uncurled his body from the blankets. He'd thought about his attraction to Tris the night before, the way he had run at the smell of Tris's blood as arousal and *wantmineneed* had stuttered through him. There was another same sex pairing within the larger pack, and the Were's attitude towards attraction was rather more simple and uncomplicated than religious teachings. Although, up to the point when he had been bitten, Euan had expected that one day he would marry, he had never felt attracted to any of the women he had met. Now he had come to terms with who he was. With the decision made, he was hoping that if he could persuade Tris, perhaps this trip could be much more pleasant.

He had removed his kilt the previous night but Tris had been curled up face to the wall and almost asleep by the time he did so. It did not escape Euan's notice that this morning Tris seemed to take an awfully long look at the length of muscular leg on display beneath the hem of his shirt. Euan grinned wider, turning to add new kindling to the remains of the fire. And if his arse happened to wiggle a bit whilst he did so, well maybe Tris shouldn't be paying such close attention.

Tris stifled a groan, dragging his eyes away from the show Euan seemed determined to give him. He turned away, ducking out the door and heading over into the trees to take care of some necessary business. He stared down at his half-hard cock, and tried to think of something unexciting enough to at least allow to him to piss in comfort. He had never been forced into such close confines with a man he found so attractive and his body was betraying him. He tried to think of some of the many unsavoury things that had filled his life recently; the smell of stables as the sun began to heat them, the small corpses that were always to be found on the stairs in one particular inn, a torn-eared tom standing smug guard over them, and the gap-toothed doxy that had tried to tempt him one damp night; but his mind kept pulling up images of wide green eyes, soft full lips curved into that half smile of amusement, firm calves and strong, tawny haired thighs.

Tris rested a hand against the tree in front of him and took his shaft in hand, working it swiftly up and down the length. The friction was just this side of too rough but he bit his lip and continued jerking hard, rubbing just under the crown on each up stroke then, as a clear liquid started to ooze from the tip, rolling his palm over the head and slicking his shaft. The possibility of Euan coming out of the small dwelling to look for him and finding Tris pleasuring himself had Tris stifling a moan, and he turned his face into the curve of his shoulder.

The image of Euan's face, eyes wide, mouth rounded in an O of surprise had his muscles tightening and Tris buried his face deeper into the curve of his arm as the sound of his release spattered against the leaves underfoot. He soothed himself through the aftershocks and finally managed to complete the business he had come out for. Tucking himself away, he fiddled nervously with his clothes before sighing softly and squaring his shoulders.

He re-entered the house feeling somewhat awkward and strangely shy to find Euan down on the floor, fastening his belt over his plaid. Euan rose to his feet and Tris watched as a couple of daggers were secreted about Euan's person. Euan smirked and then contorted himself somewhat, bringing up a corner of the kilt's material behind him and another piece in front, fastening them together at the shoulder with a simple brooch. A quick shrug and wiggle seemed to make everything comfortable and Euan turned his gaze back to Tris.

"I've no got anything to offer ye to break your fast, so why don't you just tell me who you are, what you're doing up here and how exactly you know my name."

Chapter 7

My Enemy's Enemy

Tris realised that he could stall no longer. He lifted his bag from the sleeping pallet where it had been curled between his body and the wall. Although Euan had said he had nothing to break their fast, he had still boiled water, flavouring it with spruce needles and two cups stood steaming slightly on the table. Euan had seated himself at the table, sprawled comfortably, with his eyes intent on Tris. With a sigh, Tris sat opposite and unbuckled the fastenings on his bag. Clothes were pulled out first, a spare shirt, two pairs of hose, one set of which was worn thin, and finally a box, wrapped in an oiled leather cover. Tris unwrapped the material, and set the box in front of them.

He looked up at Euan, meeting a curious, emerald stare. "I don't know if you remember, about a year ago now..." Tris trailed off nervously and Euan blinked, his brow furrowing as he thought back.

"Aye that was just before..." He cut himself off, started again. "That was the year that we tried to ransom that fat lord... couldnae even get his weight in chickens, much less in gold. By the time we sent a messenger he had fallen so far out of favour he couldnae see it if he had the eyes of a hawk." Euan chuckled at his own joke and Tris couldn't stop the small smile that curved his mouth.

"Aye, what was his name now..."

"Lord Barnard."

"Aye, that was the man."

"Do you remember the page, the one that escaped?"

"Thin boy, ducked off into the forest, brave as you please?" Euan stared at Tris as he nodded, looking down at his fingers where they toyed with the box. "That was you?" Amazement coloured Euan's

51

voice and Tris glanced up, watching as Euan looked him up and down, before Tris nodded once.

"Did you fall down a magic well or something?" Euan waved a hand, gesturing at Tris's height. "You were a wee streak of nothing. Mind you, you were the first tae ever escape from us, I'll have to give you that." Euan shook his head and chuckled. "Who would've thought?"

Tris offered another shy smile and then tapped the box gently. "Well, this is what I was carrying. I've carried it around with me ever since, force of habit I suppose. Then with everything that happened, with the changes in the king's moods and those in favour at Court and the way I've had to move about, I nearly forgot all about it. I cannot quite fathom how we have managed to meet again, perhaps you are meant to find out what this contains."

Tris shook his head, and knew the chain of events that brought him here and sat him at this table with Euan and the box sounded almost unbelievable in the bright light of day. Tris raised long eyelashes, looking back up at Euan before taking a slow sip of the warm tea. He glanced back up, and was distracted by the freckles that gilded Euan's cheekbones, revealed in the soft sunlight filtering into the hut. He was startled from his reverie, flushing as Euan slapped his hand gently on the table. A smirk curved his mouth as he said, "Well, let's find out what's in there then. Come on, lad, before I die of waiting."

Tris unfastened the small lock and let the lid fall back against the table. Both men stared at the collection of sealed missives, which were curled at the edges. The wax seals were cracked and dry. Tris removed them carefully, one by one, and laid them out in a row across the table. Underneath them all was a small lacquered case, sealed with the deep red and gold mark of the Church. A red braid spiralled around it, and for the first time Tris noticed something woven in amongst the crimson strands, a glint of white. He poked gently at it, revealing the serrated edge of a small fang.

This was the final betrayal of the trust placed in Tris by his former masters, revealing the contents to another. He could not prevent the tremble in his fingers as he reached in, even though he now felt that this was the right thing to do, some strange instinct pushing him on. Euan stretched across the table, wrapping Tris's long fingers in his.

"Why don't we leave that one to last? See what else you got here first?" Euan reached for one of the letters, pulling it in front of himself and placing one in front of Tris. He nodded at the letter. Tris reached out, carefully cracking the wax and unfolding the missive. It was a copy of a note from the king to the Earl of Mar, directing him to release monies to Sir William Alexander, Mayor of the new territory of Nova Scotia and Tris told Euan so, before Euan got a chance to look at the letter he had taken for himself.

Tris looked up at Euan, raising an eyebrow in silent enquiry, and wondered how well Euan could read, or if he could even read at all. Euan smirked slightly as he turned his gaze to the paper, and Tris got the feeling that Euan was happy to show off his ability. "Got a message to a Captain Thomas Hopkins, about the possibilities of stocking a ship, the Planter it's called. Says that money will be..." Euan looked back down at the letter, lips silently sounding out unfamiliar words. "Says that he'll get money for supplies and anything else he needs."

Although Tris already knew the contents of the letter, he didn't want Euan to know so he prompted Euan, asking, "Where is the ship sailing to?"

Euan's eyes ran over the rest of the letter. "Nov-Noveea Scoteea?" The unfamiliar words hung in the air and Tris let his eyes widen with what he hoped looked like surprise.

"Nova Scotia? That's Canada. The New World?" Tris met the older man's gaze, watching as he nodded once before his attention dropped back to the small pile of missives. The remaining letters were opened swiftly. Each letter held a copy of an official missive; detailing plans for the building and stocking of a ship, the hiring of crew and the possibility of staking a Scottish claim in the New World.

"If this is true..." Euan's words trailed off for a moment before he continued, his voice tinged with what Tris thought was hope. "If this was approved and things came tae pass as described, the ship would be sailing this year..." They both stared at the pile of letters in front of them. Tris let his gaze flicker up to the last item, sitting ominously on the table between them.

"Tris?" Euan's voice was soft as his fingers reached for the case. Tris's hand stretched across the table, pushing it into Euan's grasp. This was the one missive Tris hadn't been able to bring himself to read and now he felt like he knew why.

"You open it. I have the strangest feeling that it is for you..." Tris shook his head, still confused by this whole morning.. Euan slipped a nail under the wax seal, the small crack seeming much louder in the sudden silence of the small room. He slid several pieces of paper from the tube, a rough map of what seemed to be Scotland covered one, several places marked with a red dot, like blood spilled in drops across the country.

Euan unrolled one of the other sheets, lips moving slightly as he read slowly. This was what they had been searching for, what John had been looking for the day Euan's life had changed. And Tris had been carrying it with him all this time, unread and unknown. His face paled at the trick the Fates seemed to have played on him. His breath hitched hard as he realised that the Church elders knew everything about what they were, and also where to find them. He rolled it swiftly back up, staring hard at the map, tracing the blue trails of rivers, lips thinning as he noted the location of each drop of red. Both the map and the rest of the papers were shoved unceremoniously back in to the case, and Euan jumped to his feet, skin still pale although he could feel his anger painting crimson flags along his high cheekbones.

"Get your stuff. Now! Take all o' those," his hand waved briefly at the letters, still scattered across the table, "bring them and whatever else ye need. We have tae get tae John, we have tae..." Euan broke off, and took a deep breath. He forced himself to be calm and pulled his control around himself. He could almost feel his teeth lengthen in his mouth, and he felt the need to let the wolf out, to tear and rip and rend. But Tris was here and Tris didn't know. He didn't want to see Tris's eyes widen with fear, to see that beautiful mouth curl with disgust at the beast Euan had become.

Euan remembered his old friend Niall, and the way he had panicked, prayers spilling out of him, when Keir had revealed himself to Euan and his group. It had been the morning after the hunt which had gone awry in the strangest of ways. The wolf had chased Niall, hoping to bring him back to the encampment, but only the wolf had come back, head and tail low. Later, when Keir had become a man again, he had told them Niall had ran into the loch nearby, and had drowned himself rather than become a monster. For a long while, Euan had blamed John, but the others had all adjusted well and they survived much longer with John than they would have without him. Now his new family was under threat.

Euan just about ran from the shelter, leaving the door swinging crazily back. He heard the soft creak as one of the hinges broke free, but he could barely control his anger, his fear. Euan was halfway across the clearing by the time Tris emerged from the shelter, pacing back and forth with his head tilted as if listening for something. The sound of Tris clearing his throat had Euan whirling round, with a growl ripping from his throat. He bit it back as Tris stiffened. Worry scented the air, before there was a heavier, richer scent as Tris relaxed. His head tilted back, in what was probably an unconscious baring of the throat, a silent submission. Euan tried to smile but knew it was just a show of teeth. He stalked across the small clearing, and stopped just steps away from the younger man, while the wolf inside of him clamoured to take advantage of the offered submission, to put the other male firmly in place. Euan tried to fight against the urge, and stick to his hasty plan.

"Tris, come on. We have tae leave here, have tae get to John, to warn them..."

"What did that paper say, Euan? It was a map, I could see that, but what was..." Tris had his curiosity cut off as Euan advanced on him, fingers sliding firm against Tris's warm mouth, trapping the words inside. Why would he not just keep quiet, and do as he was told? The wolf smiled smugly. *Take him, make him submit, make him ours and then he will do as he's told.* The thought ran through Euan and he bit at the inner skin of his cheek as he tried to focus.

"I cannae tell ye now, just know that we have tae leave, that we, my clan, me and you, we're all in danger, they have been... We need tae get to John, he'll tell ye what ye need to know."

"Who's John?" The words were muffled against the calloused fingers. The soft slide of lips on skin sent sparks trailing, and Tris's cheeks flushed a soft rose. Euan slowly slid his hand away, thumb slipping and tugging slightly at the soft curve of lower lip. He groaned as the tip of Tris's tongue flickered out, licking as if to taste any traces of Euan left on his skin. The wolf howled happily as Euan lurched forward and wound a hand into the long hazel strands that curled at Tris's neck, pulling his head down to push their mouths firmly together.

He felt Tris freeze and began to pull away, but then the soft mouth opened and Tris relaxed into him. He felt the faint sigh of surrender against the heated skin of his own mouth and he deepened the kiss, tilting his head so that he could lick into the younger man's mouth. Tris tasted of sleep, but under that was something sweet, familiar and Euan chased it with his tongue, tracing the rough edge of tooth, the warm wetness of palate.

Pulling away slightly, Euan fought for control, burying his nose into the warm curve of the taller man's neck and inhaling the heady scent of autumn fruit and dark green leaves, overlaid with the salt of sweat, the faint wool aroma from Tris's cloak. He pressed his lips to the warm skin and swallowed hard. If it wasn't for the panic building in the back of his mind, and his worry for John and Ellen and Meg and the rest of his clan, he would have tumbled Tris to the soft grass below their feet, buried his nose in more intimate spots, and found out each aroused noise Tris would make, but he pulled away, his wolf pacing, frustrated in his mind.

"I'll tell ye what I can as we go, but we need tae move, now!" Euan spun and headed off into the forest, moving swift and silent through the trees. He heard Tris following behind, and wondered if he felt as confused as Euan did. He had kissed Tris. No, not just kissed him, ravaged him, his mouth felt hot and swollen and it was more than he had thought it would have been. He only wished he had picked a better time but there was no going back, only forward. They moved as quickly as they could, Euan not bothering to hide the route this time, knowing that he no longer needed to hide the location of their haven from Tris. The Church already knew.

Euan was well aware that he could have taken a more direct route if he changed forms, but he was not leaving Tris. He detoured slightly as the sun passed overhead and began to slide towards the west to pass a stream. He allowed them a pause to rest, to drink from the cool, fresh water and to share the berries that he managed to find. He could tell Tris was bursting with questions but avoided them by venturing down to the bank of the stream, then into the trees as if keeping watch. They moved off again, following the sun westwards toward the coast.

He didn't know when it happened or how or why, but he trusted Tris, not just with his life but with the lives of his friends, his family. The scent of Tris was warm in his nose, the salty, musky smell of exertion overlaid with confusion and the slight acridness of worry and underneath the tones that were distinctly Tris, a mix of bramble berries, the deep green smell of the woods in autumn, ripe with promise.

He found himself thinking about Tris's eyes, the way they seemed to change colour with his moods, his surroundings, sometimes bright and greenish gold, lit with curiosity and humour; at other times dark with sleep or contentment. Euan found himself wondering what colour they would be if he were to grab Tris and pull him in close, slide a hand up into that tumble of soft, brown hair and kiss him again, slow and deep and careful. He'd had his eyes closed, anger and fear driving him during the last kiss, but he wondered what would happen if he took it slow and deliberate, holding that hazel gaze as he nipped and licked at those soft lips.

He gave himself a mental kick, wondering when he had turned into a lassie, mooning like a love-sick girl over the colour of his sweetheart's eyes. The thought of Tris as his sweetheart brought him up short, and Tris thudded into the back of him, sending Euan tripping forward. The ground in front of Euan gave way and they both tumbled knees over ears, arse over elbow, down a steep embankment, crashing into a wall at the bottom.

A startled gasp brought Euan groggily to his knees, blood welling and dripping dark from the laceration that ran down past his eye, more blood filling his mouth from a split lip. A young soldier stood staring on the other side of the wall, blue eyes wide and round as he took in the two men bleeding into the grass. Blood trickled sluggishly down Tris's arm from a gash on his elbow, and his palms were grazed and stained green from trying to halt his headlong tumble. Euan could feel that one of his knees had been sliced open. The pain was sharp as he struggled to his feet. However, he could already feel his rapid metabolism dealing with the injuries as blood flowed to repair the wounds and new skin knitted together to cover them.

The young man's mouth opened and closed before he finally managed to yell wordlessly, then the sound of running feet came from further along the road. Another four soldiers appeared, and Euan knew that they needed to get out of there. He had already spotted the red braid attached to the boy's collar, a small cross and a wolf's tooth woven in amongst the red thread, the same symbol that had appeared at the bottom of the map, the same braid which had been wrapped around the scroll case Tris was carrying.

Chapter 8
As Time Is Running Out

Time seemed to pause for a moment, as Euan and Tris stared at the young soldier. The forest had gone still, silent except for the combined panting of their breath. The sounds of other soldiers approaching broke the stalemate. Euan knew that the older soldiers would be able tell what he was as soon as they were close enough to see that his wounds were already healing, blood clotting quickly. Even though he would scab and scar and bruise just like Tris was doing, it all moved at a swifter pace. Even whilst all this was running through Euan's mind another part of it was working out his location, working out which way to run, the best places for an ambush, the small, hidden places where he could go to ground.

He could smell salt in the air, knew that they were nearing the coast, the small inlet that curved in towards the river. The road they had tumbled onto split in two just round the bend, one curving down towards the sands, the other fork heading upwards, inland to the forests that coated the cliff tops. He knew that they could not fight, they were already outnumbered and he could smell Tris's blood, hear the drip-splatter as it trickled off the tips of his fingers. It would take too long for Tris to heal for them to attempt any kind of an ambush and even though everything that was wolf inside of Euan was screaming for a fight, he knew that they had to run and hide if they were to survive.

Quickly judging the height of the drystane dyke that bordered both sides of the road, Euan turned swiftly to Tris, pressing his mouth up against the soft curls that had tumbled down over his ears.

"I'm going tae leap the wall here and toss the young fellow back to his friends. I need ye to get over this wall and start running away from the soldiers. Follow the road until ye get tae a bend where it curves round to the left. Then ye'll need to go over the wall there on the other side of the road and down towards the sands. I'll be right behind ye."

Tris barely had time to nod an agreement before Euan was away, swinging over the wall, plaid swirling up to reveal strong legs scraped and coloured with the rust of blood and mud, along with the green of bruises and sap. His arms were reaching for the young man as Tris pulled himself together and made his own, much less dramatic, vault over the wall. He hit the ground hard, gasping as it sent a jolt of pain down his injured arm. But he pulled it in tight to his body with his other arm and he was off running, long legs settling easily into a steady lope.

He ignored the grunt of effort from Euan and the cut off yell from the young soldier, as well as the cries of surprise and anger that followed, listening only for the sound of Euan following. He heard footsteps pick up with an unsteady pace, as if Euan was favouring one of his legs, then the cries of pursuit. Tris saw the bend in the road coming up, reached out and hit the wall in front of him with his uninjured arm, swinging his body up and over, dropping and rolling on the other side, his elbow tucked in against his side for protection. He stopped, waiting until he heard the soft groan as Euan landed beside him, before they were both up and running again.

Another small group of soldiers appeared off to one side, illuminated by the setting sun as they came down from the cliff top, drawn by the sounds of pursuit. Tris slowed to let Euan move ahead of him, leading the way across the tangled mats of grasses that held the dunes together, gait lengthening as they hit the firmer sand exposed by the outgoing tide. Euan waved a hand back towards Tris and then pointed forward to the rising cliff face, its darkening surface marked with several spots of deeper blackness.

Although Tris's pulse was already pounding with the exertion of the run, he felt like he was trying to race faster yet as fear spiked through him. He really didn't want to go into any of those dark-gaped maws, and he turned his head in the vain hope that the soldiers had given up the chase. However, they still followed behind, though they had dropped back a fair bit, weighted down by the heavy leather armour and the thought that their prey was cornered. Tris shuddered but knew the caves were their only option.

Euan led Tris swiftly into one of the caves, and Tris's boots splashed softly though the small stream that continuously trickled out, trailing across the dark sands towards the sea. Tris stumbled to a halt with his arms outstretched as the faint illumination from the setting sun disappeared even more. Tris could feel his skin prickle with sweat as fear rushed through him. He was startled as Euan's strong fingers wrapped gently around his wrist. He gasped softly as he felt those warm fingers rubbing gently at the flakes of dried blood that freckled Tris's arm.

Tris felt Euan leaning in to him, pushing up slightly to place his mouth against the soft whorls of Tris's ear. "Be silent, the sound will carry far in here." The words were the faintest trickle of sound against Tris's skull, and the warm brush of breath sent a shiver chasing across his skin. The sounds of the captain ordering the soldiers to find wood for torches echoed strangely through the tunnels as if to emphasize Euan's remark.

Euan leant in again, "Come, follow me." Euan moved away from Tris into the darkness, and their only contact was the strong grip of Euan's fingers. Tris slid forwards as quietly as he could, moving closer to Euan's body, with his free hand reaching up to rest against the length of Euan's spine. Tris could feel the heat of Euan's body radiating through the thin cloth of his shirt, the feeling reassuring in the almost complete darkness.

They moved as swiftly and as silently as they could through the caves. Tris relied on the cues he could feel travelling down each arm to help him move securely through the blackness. The walls narrowed around them and Tris began to feel as if they were being slowly eaten alive by the very earth herself, and his pulse accelerated, as fear spiked through him again.

Tris heard Euan's sudden inhale, and then he slammed into the firm wall of Euan's body as he turned and stopped suddenly in front of Tris. The sudden press of Euan's body, chest to chest, stomach to stomach, meant that Tris was now the one to swiftly inhale, his breath shuddering out in a warm rush over Euan's face. They froze for a moment, both listening for sounds of pursuit, while Tris was trying to calm his breathing once more. Luckily for the two fugitives, it seemed the soldiers hadn't found the almost hidden entrance to this section of the caves. The noise they made as they searched was barely audible and no light from their torches made it through to the two men.

Tris exhaled again, calmer this time; the steady pulse of Euan's heart, his slow breaths calming him down. However, the heat of his body was now causing an entirely different feeling to curl slow and thick in the pit of his stomach. The arousal that he had pushed away earlier flooded back in and Tris let his fingers curl around Euan's wrist. Tris traced the heated pulse from Euan's wrist, trailing his fingers up the warm, soft skin of his inner arm, pushing the material of his shirt upwards to expose more of that delectable, tempting skin. His eyes closed against the darkness, and his other senses seemed to grow stronger. He heard a soft, bitten-off groan, and felt the brush of exhaled breath across his neck. Tris raised his other hand, fingers sliding over the firm curve of biceps and shoulder, tucking under the edge of Euan's collar to spread across the warm skin of Euan's neck, thumb resting in the small hollow below his Adam's apple.

Euan could feel the change in the air as Tris's fear dropped away, and he watched as his shoulders dropped back against the wall behind him, dark lashes hiding the unfocused hazel eyes. Euan was glad that the darkness hid the gold tinge to his own eyes, his wolf senses compensating as much as they could. He stifled a soft groan as the warm pressure of Tris's fingers curled around his wrist before sliding slow up his arm, bunching the fabric of his sleeve.

"Tris, what... what're ye doing?" Euan sucked in a deep breath full of the scent of rising desire, the acrid smell of fear disappearing under a flood of newer, more exciting smells. He blinked, finding his hand curled around the back of Tris's neck, fingers sliding into the soft waves of hair. Then he felt the long length of Tris's fingers trail back down his arm, wrapping around his palm and wrist before Tris pulled his hand upwards, letting it rest against the firm pectoral muscle.

"Euan..." The word sighed through the air between them, before Tris moved forward, lips brushing softly over Euan's cheek, easing down in a series of kisses that brushed against Euan's skin as soft as butterfly wings until, finally, he slid his lips gently across Euan's mouth. Tris pulled back, and Euan missed the contact almost immediately; he tried to pull his thoughts together, a sense of urgency trying to raise its head. But then Tris tilted his head and his lips pressed into Euan's once more, now slick with a sheen of saliva, sliding warmly across Euan's mouth as Tris moved against him in a tentative caress.

Cool air shivered over heated skin as Tris edged back once more. Euan opened eyes that he didn't remember closing, brain a scrambled whirl of *yesplease* and *nonotnow*. He took in the hesitant expression on Tris's face, the worry that drew tilted brows together.

"Euan?" His name was hesitant this time, still soft but questioning.

"Tris." Euan almost growled his reply, voice low with desire. He could feel the shudder that ran down the taller man's body, the restrained twitch of Tris's hips. He let another growl rumble out before he used the hand that was twisted into Tris's hair to pull his head back down, parting his lips with a steady push of his tongue. Euan licked softly at the full bottom one, sucking it between his teeth to bite at it gently, smiling against Tris's mouth as he felt Tris jerk in response.

He took full advantage of Tris's hesitance, exploring his mouth with long, slow licks, twining his tongue around Tris's, chasing the warm taste of him, before drawing back, allowing Tris his own chance to explore. He could hear as well as sense the pulse speed beneath his hand, and Euan spread his fingers wide over the firm muscle below his hand, sliding it down to tease the hardening nub of a nipple.

Euan closed his mouth over Tris's, absorbing the groan that shuddered out of him, pulling back with a low moan of his own to trail his mouth down over the long cord of Tris's neck. The slight salt tang of sweat had Euan's tongue flattening against skin and he wanted to suck and bite and lick and taste everywhere. The thought of biting Tris, of making him part of the pack, making him Euan's, flashed briefly through his mind, but he knew the bite of a full-born wolf was stronger. It would make Tris stronger. He also couldn't take the choice away from Tris; tempting as the younger man was Euan would not take anyone against their will. Instead he nuzzled at the racing pulse of the carotid artery, sealing his lips over the skin to suck blood to the surface, heated beneath his tongue. Euan let his hand continue to slide down the length of Tris's torso, then back up under his soft linen shirt. Long fingers trailed over the dips and ridges of Tris's abdominal muscles, trembling at the feel of shifting muscle as Tris's hips stuttered forward once more.

Tris let his head roll back against the hard wall of the cave, his fear of the dark, of the chase, subsumed in the swirl of want and need. The feel of strong muscle pressed against him, the slick slide of a broad, calloused palm over the skin of his stomach was so new but so familiar. His mind tried desperately to catch up with his body but his thoughts kept falling back to the same litany of *Euan want need more Euan now.* The whole day seemed to have been building towards this point, the furtive fumble in the trees, the electric kiss outside the small cabin. Now Tris wanted more and it was all he could do to swallow the pleas, keeping them safe inside where they wouldn't give his desperation away.

He tried to remind himself that Euan had basically kidnapped him, for the second time. That he was on the run from soldiers, who wouldn't have spotted him at all if Euan hadn't been force marching him across the countryside. But the other man was so close, skin heated and flush against his own body; the warm smell of sweat and arousal rising up from between their bodies. It was distracting in the best way and Tris has been lonely for so long, without family, home and he wanted, oh he wanted, and Euan seemed to want him too.

Tris felt Euan pause for a moment, his hand stilling against the warm skin of Tris's stomach, his mouth pulling away from the sensitive skin behind Tris's ear. Tris missed the touches immediately. He felt Euan suck in a harsh breath, could feel him drawing back, reining himself in through sheer force of will.

"Tris, d'ye need me tae stop?"

Tris moaned softly as the near overwhelming sense of heat and pressure and Euan pulled away. He could hear Euan speaking, asking him something. Tris focused slowly, his mind currently involved in cataloguing the hard curve of Euan's shoulder, the salty taste of his skin, the almost ticklish sensation of someone else's hand low on his stomach, moving so close to something he had never thought to have. He pulled in a slow breath as two words broke through the fog of desire.

"Yes, need!" Tris blinked slowly at the sound of his voice, low and cracked with desire. "Don't stop." The situation be damned; if he was to be captured and hanged for sodomy or whatever other reason the soldiers came up with, or sent south to crew one of the many ships that were sailing out to the Indies or even the New World, which was probably a fate worse than death, he wanted this before any chance of exploring his desire was taken from him.

His hands reached blindly out, seeking that missing warmth. He made contact with the edge of Euan's shirt, fisting the fabric and pulling Euan back towards him. He pushed a hand round to the small of Euan's back, sliding long fingers under the rolled edge of Euan's kilt. Tris pulled Euan's hips hard against his own, the sudden pressure and friction against his aching length sending the breath stuttering out of him.

He felt rather than heard Euan's answering cry, muffled against the curve of his shoulder, then Euan was twisting his fingers back into the length of Tris's hair, pulling hard to angle Tris's mouth down onto his. Where the previous kisses had been almost slow and searching, this was an assault. It was all teeth and tongue, the copper taste of blood and the slick of saliva. Tris's focus was drawn from his mouth downwards by the cool brush of air over the skin of his stomach, then his thighs, as Euan loosened the laces on his trousers, the material dropping to pool around his feet.

All thoughts of anything other than slaking his desire disappeared at the first touch of Euan's warm hand around his cock, the palm sliding rough against the sensitive skin. Euan worked Tris slow and firm, mouth trailing over the warm skin of his jaw and neck. A faint growl rolled from him as he nipped at Tris's collarbone, before returning to his mouth to lap at the soft skin, the faint taste of blood. He smiled at Tris's frustrated moan, the stuttering jerks of his hips as Tris sought more, faster, harder.

The smile faltered as Tris's hand trailed round and down, sliding futilely against the bundled thickness of Euan's kilt. Euan untangled his hand from the silk-soft strands of Tris's hair, pulled at the buckle on his hip one handed, soft curses spilling forth. Then the material was dropping to the floor to pool heavily over their feet and it was Tris's turn to curse as skin rubbed against skin. Euan pushed a muscled thigh up between Tris's legs. The pressure between his legs and the feel of Euan's cock rubbing over his hip, sliding slick against his, sent Tris spiralling over the edge, spilling his seed thick and warm over Euan's hand and his own stomach.

Tris's soft moans, the added wetness of his come, had Euan's balls pulling up tight, a warm pressure curling at the base of his spine. He pushed up into the curve of the younger man's body, his teeth gripping hard against the meat of Tris's shoulder, stifling his moan as his release pulsed through him. Only the weight of Tris's vest and shirt stopped Euan from breaking the skin. Euan pulled Tris carefully upright, stooping to redress him, fastening the lacing on his trousers with gentle fingers. Euan couldn't fight the urge to smudge his fingers through the mix of fluids coating the younger man's stomach, sucking them into his mouth with a sound that made Tris ask him what he was doing before realisation dawned.

Euan could feel the heat bloom in his lover's face, but didn't need that to sense the tumult of emotions running through the younger man, the swallowed hitch in his breath, the smell of sweat and come, the fine tremor of muscles. Euan knew that he felt some of them too, but he concentrated on the practicalities, wrapping his kilt around himself in a haphazard fashion, unable to fold it correctly in the confined space. He heard the indrawn breath, knew Tris was about to speak and Euan rubbed his thumb softly over the swollen lushness of Tris's lower lip, silencing him. He could still hear the faint sounds of the soldiers, lost in the maze of dead ends and looping tunnels behind them as he took Tris's hand. He entwined their fingers and started to lead them out into the light.

They escaped from a different entrance, pulling themselves up a narrow, sloping tunnel to emerge, like grubby butterflies from the cocoon of the earth. Tris sprawled out on the grassy cliff top, staring happily at the multitude of stars that trailed across the heavens, feeling the wide openness that surrounded him. He had never been so glad to be outside, where it did not feel as if the earth itself was about to grind him into meat paste. A deep yawn cracked his jaw and he rolled his head to see Euan drop down beside him, eyes glimmering in the faint light.

"Just need..." another yawn slid out, Tris's eyelids drooping, "... just a minute..." Long lashes closed over soft tilted eyes and a soft sleepy smile curved his lips as he felt Euan curl up behind him. Despite their short acquaintance, he trusted Euan to keep them both safe and he let sleep take him.

The pale light of dawn slid across Tris's face, waking him from his slumber. He lay still for a moment, listening to the faint sound of surf breaking on the cliff below. He turned, rolled on to his stomach and started to push himself up. As he looked blearily downhill towards the trees, his breath stuttered and he gasped as a large shape moved between the trunks. He turned to Euan, words tripping over themselves in his rising panic, ready to shake the other man awake to warn him.

"Euan, trees, something big, wolf..." Euan met his wide eyes with a sleepy emerald gaze, and his mouth curved in a slow smile, bright enough to challenge the dawn. Whatever was in Tris's mind dribbled away and his mouth hung slightly open, words lost as Euan reached over and traced a finger across the soft pout of his lower lip. Tris licked at his lips, chasing the taste of Euan's skin, leaving a slight sheen to the curve of his lower lip and Euan leaned in to press his own mouth to it, laving it with his own tongue before he hauled himself to his feet. At least he looked reluctant as he did so, which salved Tris's ego at being left there on the ground, lips parted as if waiting for more kisses.

"Come, we cannae stay here. We have to get moving, head over towards the coast. Meet up with the rest of the group. There will be some safety in numbers."

"How are we going to do that Euan? There are soldiers chasing us, the Church sent them, I could see the sigil they carried. And I'm sure I just saw a wolf in the forest, a huge one! We have no food, little water, no idea where we are..." Tris trailed off as Euan could no longer stifle his smirk, which then turned into a full on laugh, green eyes crinkling merrily, hand slapping against his thigh as Euan bent over, trying to catch his breath.

Tris waited him out, eyes narrowed. Euan finally looked over only to meet angry and confused hazel eyes. "Ah, Tris. Ye worry too much. I'll give ye the soldiers, aye and the Church too, but ye dinnae need to worry yourself about that wolf." Euan looked thoughtful for a moment before he muttered something that sounded like, "Well, not in the way you think you do." He frowned slightly before continuing.

"I know exactly where we are. Well, almost exactly, and I'm sure I can keep ye from starvation in the time it'll take us to catch up tae the rest of the clan. So on your feet."

Tris groaned, but pulled himself up, brushing grass and seeds from his clothing. He looked up to see Euan's gaze grow heated as he ran his hands over the swell of his ass, the backs of his thighs and he slowed his movements, almost caressing himself. It was Tris's turn to smirk as he watched Euan swallow hard and turn away, He could feel his dimples appearing as his grin widened and he heard Euan curse fluently before he began walking down slope, gait stiff and awkward. Tris was not used to having any power in this strange relationship and he discovered he liked it.

Chapter 9
Questions Answered

They travelled for most of the day, their pace slow as Euan guided them across the bare expanses of meadow, skirting glinting outcrops of granite, leading them mostly north and westward, following a river valley as it grew narrower, twisting back towards its source. As the light began to fade, they left the valley, moving uphill into the shelter of the trees.

"D'ye want to make a small fire?" Euan apparently thought that they had made enough distance between themselves and the band of soldiers. They had stopped in a small secluded glade, the ground carpeted with moss and grass, a small cairn and a circle of stones showing that this place had often been used as a resting point. "I'll just see if I can catch us something tae eat."

Tris blushed as his stomach growled a hungry agreement with that idea, although he had no idea how Euan intended to catch anything in the soft glow of dusk. He headed off to gather deadwood for the fire, collecting armfuls of wood and dried grasses. He also carefully selected some branches that he believed would make a makeshift spit, even though he felt Euan was overly optimistic about his chances of supplying food.

He had just got the fire started, heat blossoming as the flames licked greedily at the dried grass and twigs when he heard a soft, wet-sounding noise followed by a groan and a low-voiced curse. "Euan?" He kept his voice low, rising to a crouch, eyes sweeping across the clearing. He quietly moved in the direction of the voice, sliding ghost-like through the trees. Then, suddenly, out of the dim mists that had begun to swirl around the bases of the trunks, Euan appeared, a brace of rabbits dangling from one hand, shirt hanging over one bare shoulder, his kilt dishevelled and rucked awkwardly around his waist. Euan held up the rabbits and grinned widely.

"Dinner is served, m'lord."

Tris had no idea how Euan had found let alone caught the rabbits, their necks expertly broken, but any interest in the matter faded as the smell of cooking meat filled the clearing. They ate quickly, licking the burn of spilled juices from their fingers, before they banked the fire and curled up around it.

"Sleep Tris. We've another walk the morrow. But no so far now." Tris blinked sleepily across the low fire at Euan. His tone had changed and Tris now felt more like a companion on this strange journey, rather than a hostage or a prisoner. After all, Euan had left him alone, and left him his boots, whilst he had gone off to hunt. Tris hadn't even thought about running. His curiosity maybe had something to do with the matter, he wanted to know why Euan had sounded so perturbed over the contents of the satchel. But perhaps it also had something to do with the desire that curled in his belly every time Euan looked at him.

He thought about circling round to where Euan was curled up on the other side of the flames. This was something that he had never felt before, this yearning to be next to someone, to touch and be touched, just to hear them talk, see them smile, to make them smile. He was mostly sure that his feelings were returned but perhaps it had just been the close confines, the thrill of the chase that had led to that oh-so-pleasurable interlude in the cave, something Tris would very much like to repeat. He opened his mouth to speak but couldn't think of the words to explain himself. He had such a collection of poetry in his head, but nothing felt appropriate. As he pondered, Tris's eyes drifted closed as he yawned. The warm meat in his stomach, the sweet smell of the grasses and the burning pine lulled him into dream.

He awoke in the darkness, the fire a dim smudge of embers, skin shivering in the chill. Without really thinking about it he crawled around the remains of the fire, curling his body around Euan's, sliding an arm under the wrap of plaid draped over the slender span of Euan's waist, one leg sliding in between Euan's. His eyes had just drifted closed when he felt Euan roll to face him. He opened his eyes to find Euan's gaze searching his face, dropping to the soft swell of his lower lip before flicking back up to meet his eyes.

Tris let his tongue slide out, licking at the corner of his mouth, before he rolled his lips inwards, letting them slide out slick with saliva. Euan groaned and closed the small distance between them, kissing him softly. It wasn't enough for Tris and he parted his lips, tongue lapping at the edge of Euan's mouth, seeking the warm heat he had experienced earlier.

Just for a moment Tris thought Euan was going to pull away, but then the older man's hands came up, pushing at Tris's shoulders, flipping him onto his back before his body moved over and above, hips aligning as Euan deepened the kiss with another groan. Tris couldn't help the way his body arched up into the pressure and he felt his shaft begin to swell, his breeches quickly becoming uncomfortable. He gasped into Euan's kiss, rocking his hips upwards, chasing the friction.

He heard Euan chuckle slightly. "Patience, lad. I'll get ye there." He trailed a heated line of kisses along Tris's jaw, biting and sucking at the soft skin at the hinge, his stubble scraping against the soft skin behind Tris's ear before he moved downwards, his hands moving upwards, taking Tris's rumpled shirt with them. Euan shifted upwards onto his knees and pulled the shirt over Tris's head. Tris missed the contact and pulled Euan back down, a soft whimper escaping him as Euan's hands slid down over the tightening buds of his nipples.

Tris heard another chuckle then felt the heat of Euan's mouth as he closed his lips over one of the small nubs, tongue flicking against the taut skin, before he sucked hard and then licked over it again. Tris shuddered as the cool air hit the sensitised flesh as Euan turned his attention to the other side. Euan's mouth was replaced by his fingers, tugging and brushing, rolling the tender flesh and Tris wanted to both arch into the touch and pull away.

His whole body jerked and then froze when he felt the scrape of stubble across the skin of his stomach, followed by the warm sigh of air as Euan moaned and nuzzled his face into Tris's groin. The pressure was both amazing and startling.

"What? What are you...?"

"Hush lad. Let me, just a wee taste. Make ye feel so good Tris, I swear. Just lay back. Smell so good, bet you taste even better." Euan's fingers worked quickly at the laces fastening Tris's breeches and then once more, he was sliding them down Tris's legs. But this time, instead of the warm, firm feeling of Euan's hand closing around him, Tris felt wet heat, soft suction. His abs tightened and he blinked hard down the length of his body, wishing he could see better as Euan slowly slid his mouth down and then back up, tongue swirling round the head.

Tris collapsed back on to the ground, trying not to jerk his hips up into the hot, damp, oh so good suction. This had never happened to him before but he was sure that choking your partner was never good etiquette. He heard a slick pop and then Euan's mouth covered his again, and Tris could taste a salty bitterness to the kiss. He flushed a furious scarlet when he realised what it was he tasted.

He groaned and wound his fingers into Euan's hair, trying not to shove his head back down, but Euan must have known exactly what Tris wanted as he kissed Tris once more before whispering softly, "I was right, you taste so good."

"Oh God!" Tris couldn't swallow the small blasphemy as Euan dipped back down and sucked his length back in, swirling his tongue round the head, before running it down the length of the vein, mouthing at the small sac that was already pulling up tight to Tris's body. Euan wrapped a couple of fingers around the base of Tris's shaft and then began sucking in earnest, cheeks hollowing, fingers following his mouth on a slick of saliva and Tris's precome.

Tris felt his body tighten, shuddered as the wave seemed to move up from his feet and down his spine, heading towards the pull of Euan's mouth. He groaned and cursed and Euan pulled off with a final hard lick just beneath the head as his fingers twisted up and round the shaft. Tris convulsed and came, covering his stomach with pale sticky fluid, tremors sending his hips jerking into the cool air, the firm grip of Euan's hand.

It was a long couple of moments before Tris could react to the soft, rhythmic slapping sound and he pushed himself up on his elbows, stomach muscles fluttering with the effort. Tris moaned when the clouds parted enough to let the moon show him Euan, hard cock in hand, eyes fixed on the milky strands that coated Tris's abdomen. He blushed as the soft bulge of his own shaft twitched, trying to swell once more and it seemed that small movement was all Euan needed to bring him to completion.

A deep, low cry slipped from Euan's parted lips as his back arched and he added his own seed to the sticky mess. He fell forward, head coming to rest on Tris's chest, breath gasping over the slightly sweaty skin, as he tried to keep himself propped up on shaky arms. Tris allowed his hand to stroke over the damp skin at the nape of Euan's neck, then the hard curve of shoulder, the jut of shoulder blade.

"If the soldiers find us now, just surrender," Euan groaned and rolled onto his back. Tris felt a smile curve his lips as they lay there, fingers curled together, staring up at the darkness. He let his eyes drift shut, but then opened them as he heard Euan rise to his feet, coming back with a handful of soft dock leaves, which he used to wipe at the sticky mess. The leaves discarded, Euan dropped back down beside him and curled himself back into the heat of Tris's body, dragging the plaid over both of them. Tris sighed softly and wrapped himself around Euan once again, letting sleep taking him back into her soft embrace.

Euan must have woken first, must have slid himself carefully out from under the sprawl of Tris's limbs because Tris was aware of nothing until he felt Euan shaking his shoulder gently. He blinked up at Euan, could feel the small moue on his face at being disturbed, but Euan just smiled at him, eyes crinkling as he trailed warm fingers over the curves of Tris's arm. After a bone-creaking stretch and a visit behind some trees, Tris was ready to move out, following Euan, not focusing on the sway of the plaid material against the backs of Euan's knees, or the firm curve of calf muscles as they flexed with each step. No, it was certainly not the not-focusing that caused him to trip and slide down a small incline, landing in a wild tangle of brambles. But at least they now had handfuls of berries to break their fast.

It was just past noon when they crested a small rise, looking down into a long valley, a river tumbling its way through, descending in cascades of glittering rainbow spray over several falls. Hidden amongst the trees were several small shelters and a couple of cleared plots, sprouting with vegetables, chickens clucking happily amidst the leaves.

They descended the slope, making their way carefully across a sprawl of damp stones, the water gurgling merrily past their feet. Almost as soon as Euan set foot on the other side of the river, a young woman came running out from one of the shelters, long skirts gathered up into her small hands, flashing glimpses of slender calves, her blonde hair flying behind her. She leapt into Euan's arms, face buried in the curve of Euan's neck, a muffled blur of words falling from soft pink lips.

Euan staggered slightly under the onslaught, but caught the female, arms wrapping around her as he sent a look over to Tris. Euan's expression was a mix of surprise and embarrassment that turned somewhat fond as he set the woman back on her feet, hands petting her shoulders. Tris heard footsteps and turned to see an older woman approaching, shaking her head in mock dismay before she sent a sharp, white grin in Tris's direction.

Smiling at them both, Euan turned to the young woman first, "Did I no tell ye that it would all be fine, Meg?" He tweaked one of the small braids that held back the front edges of her hair and turned to the other arrival. "D'ye no have any control over this wayward daughter o' yours?" The older woman laughed at the second comment, shaking her head fondly.

"Ye know Meg has always been a law unto herself. What makes ye think she's going to change now?" The young woman mock pouted, before she rose onto her tiptoes to peek over Euan's shoulder, looking Tris up and down.

"You bought me a present?" She bared her teeth in a wide smile at Tris, gaze hungry.

"Uh-uh. He's no for you, darling. So hands off." Tris couldn't see the look that passed between them, but he could feel the air prickle with tension, could see Meg jerk back, nose wrinkling, and could see the smile that widened on the older woman's face, as she stepped closer to Euan. Tris stood awkwardly as the trio seemed to have a silent conversation, a quick argument consisting of traded glances and changes in posture. Finally, Euan stepped back towards Tris, Meg dropped her gaze in grudged submission and the older woman sent

Tris another enigmatic smile.

Euan reached out and wrapped strong fingers around Tris's wrist, pulling him forward. "Tris, this is the lovely Lady Ellen and her daughter Margaret. Don't believe anything they tell you about me." Tris smiled politely at them, bowing low over Ellen's hand, and nodding at Meg.

"Meg, would ye be kind enough tae fetch Tris a drink, perhaps take him tae the main hall if there's still some food around?"

Meg nodded, flicking a glance up at Tris from under her lashes. "Are you sure I cannae..." Meg's question trailed off at the fierce look from Euan and she turned to lead Tris towards a larger structure tucked in amongst the sheltering trees. Tris sent a single glance backwards as he was hustled away, to see Euan and Ellen already deep in conversation, faces grim.

It was nearly nightfall when Euan came back. Men had been trickling into the small encampment throughout the day, some wounded, others healthy but showing signs of exhaustion. Tris had been helping Meg, ripping up sheets for bandages, fetching water from the river, firewood from the piles dotted throughout the trees. He had found the young woman surprisingly funny, her wit sharp and biting as she provided aid and assistance wherever she was needed.

Now Tris was finally sitting, slumping against the wall of one of the small buildings, legs stretched out in front, picking tiredly at a small bowl of some kind of stew. He passed it to Euan as he dropped heavily down beside him, offering him the hunk of bread that was sitting wrapped in cloth next to him. "I don't know if you've already eaten, but..." Tris trailed off, flicking nervous glances at Euan before glancing away into the woods and back again.

Euan took the bowl with a grateful smile, picking out the chunks of unidentifiable meat, swallowing them almost whole. He crammed a large chunk of bread into his mouth, chasing it down with a gulp of water from the flask he'd brought over. He offered the water to Tris before gulping down the rest of the stew. After chasing the remains of the meaty sauce with the final piece of bread, Euan dropped the bowl carelessly to the ground, pulling himself back to his feet with a low groan. He held out a hand to Tris.

"John wants tae meet ye. Things are coming to a head and, well, there's..." Euan trailed off awkwardly, looking hesitant and for the first time unsure of himself. "Aye, well, anyway, we'd better no keep John waiting."

Tris let Euan hoist him to his feet and followed as Euan led him along a path through the small shelters until they arrived at one of the biggest ones there. It seemed a lot more solid, better built than the rest, the stone walls were weathered, and the door was stiff with age. Inside, it was split into two rooms, a door leading through into what was probably the bedroom. The room they were in was well lit with candles and the warm glow from the fire that burned in a large hearth. A table took up most of the room, the delicate carving showing the same hand as the furniture from the other cabin. Tris briefly wondered if it was the man seated in front of them that was responsible.

Dark eyes observed them carefully, the man's face guarded and still as he watched them enter. Tris couldn't decide how old he was. Older than Euan, but he couldn't tell by how much. His dark beard was slightly greying yet his hair was still dark. His eyes crinkled at the corners, showing the signs of a life spent outdoors, arms tanned and solid with muscle. His gaze however seemed older, laden with sorrow and worry. "Euan." The man's voice was gruff, his hand waving them both to a seat.

Tris had been concentrating so hard on John that he almost missed the way Euan stiffened, the abortive movement towards John, his hand stilling before it reached out. He did see the way Euan's eyes darkened with worry, his lip curling back almost as if he smelt something unpleasant. They sat at the table, Tris awkward and stiff in the unfamiliar setting, Euan tense and worried. Ellen came in carrying wine and cups enough for each of them and the two men that followed.

"Tris, this is Lachlan, Robert, and you've met Ellen." Tris nodded to the two men, watching as they took seats as well. The younger man, Lachlan, slim with light hair and pale eyes stirred a memory in Tris and it took a moment before he placed him with Euan, that day long ago. He took a spot to the right of Euan whilst the man introduced as

Robert moved round behind John, his brow furrowed as he took his place beside John. Robert seemed to be possibly older than John, his beard mostly grey with only traces of its original dark auburn hue. His face was creased with worry, life leaving its marks across his skin.

All the men were in kilts, woven in various shades of heather and brown and green and plain linen shirts. Each was armed, daggers stuck in the woollen socks that covered their calves, tucked into belts. Lachlan had a short sword strapped to his spine.

John brought Tris's attention back to the small, cramped room with a gruff request, "Report." He studied John as the older man watched Euan relating his tale of finding Tris in the woods after he left the inn, about the soldiers finding them, or rather them almost falling directly into the troop. He ran through the details quickly, John nodding at points. Thankfully, he left out any of the more personal events.

It was Robert who broke the silence at the end, hand rubbing at his beard as he sent a probing look at Tris, inhaling deep as he leant forward, broad scarred hands pressing against the tabletop.

"So ye think that..."

Euan cut him off, "Tris, show them the letters." Tris blinked at the curtness of Euan's tone, but pulled out the box of letters and the scroll case, placing them both on the table, pushing them slightly towards the other men.

Everyone's gaze dropped immediately to the case, Robert tentatively reaching a finger out towards the red braid wrapped around it before pulling back, almost as if it would burn him. "Did ye...?"

The question came from two sides, Robert and Ellen both looking at Euan and then John before their gazes dropped back to the case. Tris wondered what exactly the contents meant to the group, what made it so unsettling to them. Euan nodded once and reached out again to the case, pulling the papers out into the soft light. He spread the map on the table, weighting the corners with the small pebbles that had obviously been used for that purpose before. Euan passed the other sheets of paper to John, who unrolled them, gaze running swiftly over the pages, his skin blanching to a sickly grey.

Ellen had slid round behind him, reading over his shoulder, her fingers curled softly round John's shoulders. One hand rose to her mouth as her eyes widened in what was either fear or shock. Robert swore gently but profusely, the sentiment echoed by Lachlan as he finally got a look at the papers. Tris blinked as five pairs of eyes turned to him, fighting hard against the urge to back slowly out of the room before turning and running and never stopping.

Chapter 10

Revelations

"Where and when did ye get this, son? And who are you?" The questions were soft, and John's voice was thick with fatigue. Tris told the group, explained that it should have been passed to a contact that was to meet him at the Keep in the Borders just over a year ago. That it had been sent from the Cathedral in York. He told them that he was just a simple page, picked because no-one would have looked at him twice.

"That's probably the only reason we're still here. We have managed tae intercept other messages, including one that Lachlan brought back with him, but none as detailed as this one. If this had been passed on a year ago, we surely would have been found and our Clan would be no more. We owe ye thanks. Why did ye no take it to the Church as ye had been told?"

Tris met John's dark eyes, and then glanced quickly at Euan before he cleared his throat and said softly "The Church has not been the most welcoming place of late. I had been going to return, but some of the things I saw, the things I heard from others.... And then I had left it so long it seemed like I had made it even more suspicious. I knew they would wonder how only I had gotten free, where I had been, had I been captured, turned, bribed?"

Tris looked at the small group, noting the consideration in their eyes, the small nods of acknowledgement and he looked back at the map as the others returned their gazes to it. He wondered if he would finally get an explanation, turned an enquiring gaze towards John. John noted the look and pointed to the map, still spread on the table.

"It shows every place our Clan and others like us have homes.

We're here," John let a finger rest on a small dot, just under a blue line that curved its way towards the sea on the west side of the drawing. "This was our original home," his finger pointed to another location further south and Tris realised that this would be near where Lord Barnard and his entourage were heading when he had first met Euan.

"Why are you so important to them? I don't mean to offend but you do not seem like a highly organised resistance force." Tristan was still confused. John's gaze flicked to Robert, who nodded slightly. Ellen let her hand slide down over John's chest, resting her fingers over his heart, a silent symbol of support and so much more. John then turned to Euan, an eyebrow raised in silent question. Tris held his breath, feeling that the whole future was hanging on Euan's response.

Euan stared at Tris for a moment before he turned back to John, nodding and flushing pink at the knowing glances and smirks that were now curving everyone's lips. Tris's gaze flickered around the table, knowing that some kind of decision had been made, knowing that Euan was somehow amusing the group, but he had missed the punch-line completely.

"I take it that Euan hasnae told ye much about our wee group?" Tris shook his head. "Well, ye've probably gathered that we're no exactly welcome in these parts, especially with the Church. We've tried our best tae live in harmony, tae keep ourselves hidden, but the king is involved now and it's time for us tae move on. This ship..." John waved his hand over the papers, "is our best hope, our chance for a new beginning, for our clan tae live in peace and safety."

Tris nodded. "But why? I mean, why the Church, all the soldiers... and what does the map and..." His question ran out of steam in the middle, confusion and worry colouring the words. John coughed wetly, the sound painful in the silence and looked at Euan. Euan rubbed his hand slowly over his face before he slid his chair round, so that he was facing Tris more directly.

"The map shows all of our safe havens, every shelter we have, our homes, the village here. The paper...it explains what we are. It is the Church's declaration that we are an abomination. It says that that we need to be wiped from the face of the Earth, that the soldiers have permission to show no mercy to our Clan, to our women, our children. It tells them how we can be killed."

Tris looked around once more, seeing the worry and fatigue that marked each face, the anger that simmered beneath Lachlan's laid back demeanour, the sadness on Ellen's face as she leant against the man she obviously loved dearly. He turned back to Euan, his voice plaintive as he asked, "But why? Why you?" For some reason, the thought that so many people bear such ill-will towards Euan made his heart clench in fear and also anger. He watched as Euan flicked another glance back towards John before he cleared his throat, lips twisting as he tried to work out what he wanted, what he needed, to say.

"John found us about a year ago. Just after we had captured Lord Barnard. John had realised that the Church had found out about them and had decided to deal with the... the problem, once and for all. The Church had been ignoring them up until then, aware, but perhaps hoping that the problem would go away, or maybe they were hoping to turn things to their advantage in some way. But then the king had obviously been hearing rumours too, had decided that this was not to be some Godless, heathen country, full of renegades. He wanted them to kneel and they would not submit."

John grinned slightly at this comment but didn't interrupt. Euan continued, "My wee clan hadn't been doing too well, I'd been losing men, tae the cold, tae hunger and of course the skirmishes that were always going on. Then our ransom attempt failed badly." He shot a quick smile at Tris. "We'd been out hunting, me and some of the other men, we'd found a deer, hadnae realised that it was..." Euan coughed, smothered a soft smile, "somebody else's kill. John, Ellen and Meg chased us down..." Euan paused again as Tris raised a surprised eyebrow.

"You were captured by girls?"

Ellen laughed at Euan's affronted face, before she turned to Tris. "Well, tae be fair to Euan, we were armed with some rather unusual weapons." She laughed again, Robert and John smirking broadly beside her, Lachlan desperately trying to disguise his laughter as a coughing fit. Euan rubbed his hand over his face, muffling the groan before his hand moved round behind his neck to rub at the skin there, and Tris realised that Euan was nervous, was worried about telling Tris whatever it was he was trying to get out.

"Aye, unusual is no even the word for it." Euan gave a bark of a laugh, his lips curving at the memory. "They split us up, took out my men first, cornered me and then made me an offer I couldnae really refuse. And so we became part of John's clan."

Lachlan nodded agreement, "Euan came back tae camp, there wasnae many of us left then, but we moved up here, those of us who were able enough were..." Lachlan trailed off too, sending another glance at Euan, who sighed wearily, surrendering.

"Mebbe it would just be easier to show him?"

Tris watched as Euan's gaze flickered nervously once more around the group. He'd never seen Euan so unsettled. He'd always been composed, cocky even, whether they were just walking or being chased. "Show me what?"

"It's up to you son, but we dinnae have much time." John spoke at the same time as Tris, his voice low, as he shifted in his seat, face twisting somewhat. Perhaps he was injured, like many of the men in Euan's clan. Euan rubbed his hands over his face again, before his shoulders stiffened in decision and he rose to his feet.

"Tris, please, whatever ye do, don't run. Promise me you won't run."

Tris stared at Euan, wondering how much stranger this night was going to get, and startled as Euan reached out to wrap strong fingers around his arm, green eyes looking searchingly at him. He met that worried gaze and the world seemed to fade out around him, going indistinct and pale compared to that emerald stare, the gilded freckles that spattered the skin around it. He sucked in a suddenly shaky breath.

"Y-yes. I... I promise. I'll stay right here." He patted the curved wood of the seat, as if to emphasise the point, then blinked in surprise as Euan turned and walked out the door. Lachlan moved round beside him as Robert moved towards the door, taking up a stance beside the worn wood. Tris's brows drew down as he frowned, his worry increasing as he heard a soft pained sound from outside, recognising the low tone.

"Euan..."

He tried to rise but Lachlan clamped a hand down on his shoulder, the grip surprisingly strong. Tris could almost feel the bone in his shoulder creak at the abuse.

"Not so hard Lachlan, I don't think Euan would like you marking up what's his." Ellen grinned sharply at Lachlan, who relaxed his hold a little but left his hand resting heavy on Tris's shoulder. The door creaked slightly, and everyone's gaze spun towards it like filings drawn to a magnet. It eased slowly open, and Tris's jaw echoed the movement as one of the biggest wolves he had ever seen padded slowly into the room.

Tris's gaze flickered around the room. None of the others seemed to be bothered by the fact that there was now a wolf slowly walking towards Tris, tongue lolling loose and pink over razor sharp teeth. Tris dragged his gaze away from the glint of fang, pulling it up to meet an amused gold gaze. He stared at the wolf, at the eyes, leaning forward in his chair as the wolf moved closer still, claws ticking gently on the wooden floor.

Gold eyes with flecks of green, almost a reverse image of...

"Euan?" Tris's voice squeaked awkwardly, his pale cheeks colouring a soft shade of pink as he pulled in a sharp breath and reached out tentatively towards the animal. The wolf dropped to its haunches in front of Tris, before it stretched forward to rest its head heavily in Tris's lap. Tris curled his fingers into the ruff of auburn tinted fur, sliding them up over the velvet soft skin of a forward tilted ear.

The wolf turned its head, long tongue licking softly across the tender skin of Tris's inner wrist, teeth grazing the delicate skin. Tris shuddered, the fear fading, replaced by awe and wonder.

"But how?" Tris coughed as his voice cracked again. "Are you all...?" His gaze skittered over the group, noting the soft smile on Ellen's face, the pride on John's, the smirk that only broadened as he met Lachlan's eyes as he slumped back down into his seat. John sucked in a breath to answer but Robert moved back from his position by the door, motioning John backwards, letting him rest.

"John is our Ceann-fine, the wolf in charge if ye will. He's also a born Were, same as me and Ellen and Meg. Yer man Euan and Lachlan over there, they're bitten Weres, same as most o' the other men out there. Makes a difference to what they can do, but basically we're all wolves under the skin. The offer on the table is: join us and come tae the ship with us, or we'll take ye out in the hills somewhere, drop ye off and ye can take yer chances getting back tae a town."

Tris stared down at Euan, the golden eyes fixed on his face, and then turned back to the others. "Do I have to say right now? It's so much... too much... and you can..." His voice stuttered away to nothing and he could feel teeth grip his arm gently and tug. Rising to his feet Tris followed the wolf, followed Euan, towards the door as Ellen hushed the men, waving them back to their seats whilst turning a soft smile on Tris as he stumbled out the door.

Tris let the wolf pull him back to the small building he had been sitting outside earlier, his whole world view spinning around him. The only thing that kept him grounded was the soft pressure of teeth against the tender skin of his arm, the warm huff of breath over the skin, the bump of the solid body against his thigh and hip. The wolf dropped his arm, nudging him towards the door and Tris managed to force his shaking legs to walk him inside before he finally crashed to the ground, his hands rising up to cover his face as he gasped for air.

Tris heard the wolf walking into the small room behind him, but he just curled his arms tighter around himself, burying his face against his knees. He squeezed his eyes closed, but it did not prevent the slow trickle of salt tears as the events of the past few days finally caught up with him. Euan padded silently over to drop to the floor beside the young man, his large head nudging gently at the young man's shoulder, a soft whine sounding in his throat. Tris uncurled and buried his damp face in the thick ruff of fur that covered Euan's neck, arms circling the wolf as he worked through the emotions that had piled up over the past days. He had fled an attack, been captured, and marched across the country by a man who he seemed to be falling in love with at an almost ridiculous rate. And now he had found out that the person he had wanted to give himself to was not even human, and was under a death threat from both the king and Church.

He knew that he needed to think about this, about what he would be giving up, about what he could gain but he had just been so afraid for so long. Right now Tris felt no fear. He knew that the wolf would not hurt him, that the wolf was as much Euan as was the man and he curled himself into the warm, furry body, taking comfort from the steady heartbeat, the soft huffs of breath that stirred the hair at the nape of his neck. The wolf pulled away, nosing at Tris's neck quickly before he licked at the trails left by the tears that had tracked down Tris's face. Tris squeaked in surprise and pushed at the wolf's shoulder, swiping at his own face.

"No, no licking, that's just.... Bad wolf." Tris blinked, still trying to take it in and he asked tentatively, "Could you change back? I really need to see Euan just now. I mean, I know that you are Euan, too, or that Euan is in there somewhere, or... I don't know at all how this works, but I need the Euan I know, the one that can talk to me. Please?"

Euan slipped outside and forced himself to change back. He had changed too much in a short space of time and this one hurt, so much more than usual, but Tris had asked to see him and he finished the change with a low cry of pain. Someone had left his shirt and plaid outside the door and he wrapped the warm wool around his shuddering body gratefully. Staggering to stand on legs as shaky as a new born lamb's, he stumbled back into his small home.

Euan dropped gracelessly to the floor behind Tris and pulled him back against his chest, hands just resting against the soft swell of Tris's upper arms, fingers drawing meaningless swirls and stripes. He sat and let Tris lean against him, drawing comfort from the solid strength as he let go of the fear and confusion in a few more soft, snuffling gasps. Finally, Tris's breathing settled into a more normal rhythm and he turned his face towards Euan, burying his face in the curve of Euan's neck, his hand rising to lie gently over Euan's heart. Euan wrapped his arms firmly around Tris, realising that for all of Tris's height and muscle he was still a young man, sheltered by the Church and the lords into whose service he had been given.

"So... does... does it hurt?"

The question was plaintive, almost childlike, and Euan smiled into Tris's hair, soothed by the soft scent of brambles and heather that was distinctively Tris.

"Being turned? Aye, aye it does. The only way it can be done is by bite and there's nae way tae make it any more pleasant. But I'll be with ye, right beside ye, and when it's done you'll be able tae see the world in such a different way. And ye can come with us, with me... if... if that's what ye'd like?" Euan's voice was soft as he voiced the last question, worried that now Tris had seen what he was, he would want nothing more than to get as far away from Euan as possible. His breath hitched in his lungs as he waited for an answer.

Euan turned so that he could look at Tris, eyes flickering over the soft golden skin, the tip-tilted eyes. He watched Tris's skin flush as his eyes trailed downwards over the wide expanse of shoulder, the firm chest and he knew that he was right to offer Tris the choice. He needed to let him make the decision, and he hoped with all his heart that Tris chose them, chose him. They hadn't made anyone else part of the pack since they had turned Euan, trying to keep their group small enough to avoid notice. He hoped that they would accept Tris.

Tris's hand spread wide over Euan's chest, fingers sliding against the damp skin as his mouth nuzzled gently at Euan's neck. Euan held himself still, let Tris work through his decision in his own time. He wondered what his thoughts were as he sat curled in Euan's lap, fingers resting softly over Euan's heart. He felt Tris pull in a deep breath, shuddered slightly as Tris blew it out, the warm air rushing over his bare chest. He felt Tris's hand drop from his chest before it planted itself firmly on Euan's thigh. Tris bracing his body as he leant back to meet Euan's worried gaze. Euan held his breath, waiting.

"Yes. Yes, I'd like that." Tris offered the words tentatively at first, but his voice was strengthening as he finished the sentence, resolution filling that hazel gaze. A small smile curled the edges of his lips.

Euan stared at him for a moment before his lips curved upwards in a smile that he could not hold back. A low growl rumbled its way out of Euan's chest and he tightened his arms around Tris, pulling him close. Euan pressed his smile against Tris's neck, trailing kisses upwards, murmuring "mine" and "leannan" amidst the soft sounds of kisses. Fate had brought him to Euan for a second time and even though Euan was an outlaw and an honest-to-God mythical creature, he realised that Tris appeared to have no problem whatsoever with the matter. Tris's dimples flashed briefly before they were swallowed up by a large yawn. His cheeks flushed pink again, the colour deepening at Euan's smirk. Now he had started he couldn't seem to stop and another yawn rippled through him, however, he did manage to hide that one behind his hand. Euan pressed a soft kiss to Tris's forehead before he dragged himself to his feet, muscles still aching. He had never changed so much in such a short period. He pulled Tris up and guided him over to the pile of blankets tucked against the far wall.

Tris's eyes were drooping badly and he let Euan guide him down into the bed, trying to voice a protest as Euan pulled his boots off. "Can do it 'self..."

"Let me. Let me take care of you." Euan smiled as Tris flailed slightly before dropping back down. He tucked Tris under the blankets, eyes soft with an emotion he didn't want to name. Another kiss was ghosted over Tris's forehead and Euan wrapped the younger man in his arms pulling him tight against his body. He buried his nose into the side of Tris's body, inhaling deep, his inner wolf slumped with satisfaction. "Sleep, leannan." he murmured and he slept as well, his sweetheart safe in his arms.

Chapter 11

Endings and Beginnings

Euan wasn't sure exactly what had awoken him. He laid still, nostrils flaring, scenting the air. There was the faint scent of pine smoke from the fire, fading like the glowing embers; the delicious smell of Tris, blood heat and sweat, warm wool from the blankets wrapped round him. His head turned slowly, there it was – the faint jingle of harness, soft sound of feet.

Euan rose silently from his bed, moving swift across the room to collect his weapons before he moved back, hand clamping down hard over Tris's mouth as he woke him, cautioning him to silence. Euan passed Tris a dagger, edges glinting in the last glimmers of firelight before he tucked another one into his belt and pulled his sword from under the sleeping pallet.

Another hand motion, signalling Tris to wait there as Euan slipped, sleek and silent still, through the window, sliding from shadow to shadow. Eyes shifted, pupils enlarging to catch the traces of movement in the trees, the glint of starlight on steel.

A familiar scent curled round him, Lachlan moving up beside him, John close behind. A wordless conversation, darted glances, discreet hand movements, a plan agreed. Lachlan faded back into the night towards the other shelters. There was the thick wet sound of flesh reshaping itself, the creak and pop of bones and ligaments shifting, a stifled moan. Then the soft sound of panted breath, the brush of thick fur against the skin of his lower arm. Euan looked down to see the lupine version of John's smile, a dark gesture full of sharp malevolence, before the wolf slipped ghostlike into the night.

Euan shifted his sword from hand to hand, taking comfort from the weight of the blade, the cool reassurance of the steel as he edged himself into position. Then the night erupted as soldiers and horses plunged from the trees, steel glinting in the moonlight. Torches were thrown, the summer-dried sod of the roof next to him catching fire, the flames adding a hellish tint of colour to the moonlit scene.

Euan spun on one foot, the other planted solidly on the ground behind him as he raised his sword. He caught a mounted soldier on the arm, blood spraying black in the night air as he continued the movement, sword pulling back and down towards his left hip, before he twisted at the hip, pushing the sword up and to the right, sliding it through flesh, grating against bone.

Thick scent of warm copper and then a darker scent filled the air as the soldier toppled from his horse, guts exposed as Euan's sword slid free. Euan pirouetted again just in time to receive the hilt of a sword to the face. He felt the skin tear, blood trickling down over one high cheekbone. He blinked, trying to clear his vision, raising his sword again instinctively. He heard the ringing sound of metal on metal, then the smell of fresh blood and the warm, bramble scent that was distinctively Tris.

Wiping the blood from his eye, he could see Tris staring at him. A body sprawled at Tris's feet, Tris's dagger and his hand were stained red with blood. Euan saw the shudder run through Tris, and could see that his eyes were wide, hazel colour almost drowned by the black, as he stared at the man he had just killed. The first man he had killed judging by his reaction. Euan's breath caught in his throat as he wondered whether Tris was about to turn tail and run, or stand his ground. Tris stared down at the body and then back up at Euan.

Time seemed to slow around them; the harsh sounds of steel, the worrying crackle of fire almost fading into the wind. Euan found he could not look away from the moment that would decide his lover's fate. He waited for Tris to make his decision, knowing they had barely any time for Tris to process the situation.

Euan could almost see the emotions run through him, could certainly smell the fear, and something that made Euan think of a mother protecting her cubs, a sense of righteous anger. Then the decision was made, and Tris stepped up to Euan, one arm pulling him tight against his body for a brief moment before they broke apart, moving as one toward the sounds of battle.

Tris blinked hard as he followed Euan, wondering when and if his heart would ever settle back into its previous rhythm. The fire spread, leaping in sparkling trails of wind-blown embers from roof to roof. The new flames were caught, smothered under damp woollen blankets and dark handfuls of earth. Tris kept his eyes averted in an attempt to protect his night vision. A figure loomed out of the dark, his face twisted with anger, steel swinging in a wide arc.

Euan slid out of the way; a graceful curve of spine, dip of hips and bend of legs. Tris and Euan lunged as one. Tris's dagger slid past the man's throat as Euan's went slicing deep through the back of the man's legs. The figure collapsed like a marionette with severed strings, blood pooling dark and thick beneath him. They shared a brief smile, Euan's wide and sharp, Tris's full of relief before they resumed their hunt.

The unexpected sound of laughter brought Tris's head round to find Meg, seemingly backed up against the wall of John's house, two soldiers advancing slowly towards her. Two bodies lay behind them and sadness filled Euan as he recognised Maeve and Connor. Connor's head had been struck from his body, Maeve was lying on her stomach, a large rip in her dress and the thick spill of blood showing where she had been attacked from behind as she tried to flee.

"We've caught ourselves a right pretty one here." Laughter echoed again, dark and wicked, as the soldiers exchanged glances. "It'd be a shame to mark such a pretty face, so why don't you spread your legs like the whore you are and maybe we'll let you... escape... once we've had our fill." The taller of the two dropped his hands to the laces of his trousers, the other tossing a dagger from hand to hand.

Tris felt Euan slide a muscled arm around his waist, pulling him back into the shadows, mouth pressing to Tris's ear. "Tis all right, leannan. Why don't we let the fair Meg show these gentleman the error of their ways? Cannae take all the fun to ourselves. How about we just wait here, just in case she does need our assistance?" Tris tried to ignore the shiver than ran over his skin, the feel of Euan's body pressed tight along the length of his spine, as he watched Meg ease her small pale hands behind her back, eyes falling closed.

"Open your eyes, pretty. So you can see what you're getting." The two men were close enough to touch but Meg stayed still, pressed up against the wall, eyes closed. Tris wondered why he didn't think her eyes were closed in fear, then he realised. Meg was still, her slender body poised gracefully, no tremors or shivers of fear shook her small frame. A small smile began to curve the soft lips.

"I said, open your eyes, whore!" The taller man's arm swung round, a back-handed slap towards Meg's face that never made contact. Meg's eyes flicked open, flashing in the dim light as her grin widened and her hands came from behind her back, her left arm catching the swing, the other pushing forward into her assailant's stomach.

It was a decent punch, but it shouldn't have brought the scream that ripped from his throat, shouldn't have his eyes widening in pain and fear as Meg moved in close. Tris could see her lips move, but could not catch the words. However, he certainly understood the intention as Meg spat in the man's face before sliding out of his grasp and turning on his companion. He crumpled to the ground behind her, clutching at the darkness that spilled from his abdomen.

"Come on then, lover, don't ye want to play anymore?" Meg's smile seemed to be too sharp, her hands dripping red as she advanced on the remaining soldier. She turned, a small smile directed at Euan and Tris where they stood in the shadows, before she went back to her prey.

Euan pulled Tris back into the night, away from the sound of wrenching gasps, a cut-off burble of a scream. Tris looked enquiringly at Euan and he matched Meg's wolfish grin as he explained, "Ye ken how Meg's a full born wolf? Well, one of the things that makes them better is that they can control their shifting a lot more; she's been doing it since she was a bairn. So if Meg feels like it, she can be a pretty, innocent-looking maid – with a mouth full of fangs and razor sharp claws."

The night flickered red around them, figures looming out of the smoke and shadows, before fading back, pained cries and battle screams echoing oddly in the darkness as they slipped between trees and sheltering walls. Euan knew that they were outnumbered, that they needed to withdraw, their sanctuary beyond redemption. He needed to find John, to get his leader's permission to withdraw. He hoped that Lachlan had already managed to get the children to safety, that John had warned the rest of the men that the soldiers had silver coated weapons, that any cut would prove extremely painful and almost incapacitating. Euan saw another wolf fall to a silver blade and took the soldier down with a guttural growl of fury.

He found Ellen first, her hands and arms painted dark with blood and grime, bruises beginning to mottle her cheek, her mouth bleeding. "Where's John? We need tae pull back, the clan cannae take these kind o' losses."

Ellen nodded in agreement and Euan relaxed slightly, the female's support easing some of the worry that filled his chest. "Where's Meg? We'll gather the others, start heading for the trees, once we can shift they'll no be able tae track us."

Euan pointed back the way they came, "She's back there, a couple of soldiers seemed tae think that she would provide some entertainment. Dinnae think they got what they were expecting."

Ellen smiled darkly, muttering about men never learning. "Oh, I've learnt." Euan grinned just as dark, gallows humour, before raising an eyebrow in silent question.

Ellen sighed softly before answering. "The last I saw of John, he was heading towards the main hall, trying tae lead some of the soldiers away from me. Euan, ye need tae find him, soon!" Ellen's plea brought a frown to Euan's face, and he reached out to run a hand soothingly down her arm.

"Euan, ye need tae find him, ye need tae take Tris to him. We have nae time left for thinking about things, it has tae be done, John... John is..." Ellen's voice trailed off, tears pooling, then falling in silent crystal drops to mix with the blood that trailed across her cheekbones. Euan already knew, he could smell it earlier, the thick scent of old blood, flesh gone bad. He turned to Tris before spinning back and pulling Ellen into a hard, brief hug. He brushed a thumb gently over one cheekbone, catching tears and blood.

"I'll tell him."

"He knows."

Ellen turned and fled, her form devoured swiftly by the drifting smoke. Euan turned back to Tris, wrapping a hand round his wrist and pulling him stumbling and tripping through the dark and smoke towards the heat and flames, the main hall now beyond saving, the clan's haven drifting off on the breeze in flickering sparks and soft, choking clouds of ash.

They found John down beside the river, still in his wolf form, thick dark fur making him almost invisible in the dark. Several bodies were lying on the bank beside him, blood spilling into the dark flow of water. John's muzzle was stained with blood, his thick, dark fur spattered and sticky with fluid. He turned dark eyes on Tris and Euan, waiting, silent apart from his soft panted breaths. Tris nodded once, answering the unvoiced question, before he pulled his shirt over his head, Euan echoed the nod and John huffed out a larger breath.

Euan pulled Tris down to the ground, their knees sinking into the soft soil. Wrapping strong arms around his waist, Euan turned Tris until his shoulder was offered to John. John slunk slowly towards them, his front left leg barely touching the ground as he moved, the fur matted dark, paw hanging limp. Tris shivered as the cold air brought goosebumps to his skin and he curled towards Euan's warmth, but then Euan shook him, almost like a rag-doll, and the movement had John darting forward, teeth sinking hard into the meaty flesh of Tris's upper arm.

Tris sucked in a breath, eyes opening wide in startled hurt as he tried to jerk his arm away from the sharp pain. Euan held him steady, preventing him from pulling away until a scream finally broke free from Tris. Euan held him still as John finally pulled back, watched as John licked over the bite mark, ensuring that it was well coated in saliva. Tris's back arched as the pain rippled through him, his cries trailing off as he slipped into unconsciousness. Euan let Tris rest gently against his chest as John forced himself through one final change.

Faint sounds of fighting echoed from the dark as Euan busied himself with making Tris comfortable against the chill earth, one hand over the hard beat of his heart, feeling for the steadying rise and fall of his breath. He added his own soft licks to the bite mark as he waited for the hurtful damp crunches and gasps of pain from behind him to slow and cease.

"Euan."

The whisper had him spinning round, had him crawling over to John's side, head low in submission and desperate love. His eyes lifted reluctantly, moving up over the dark gash in John's side that still showed no sign of healing. He could see the hand hanging limp, the arm still slowly trickling blood from a slice that should have been scarring over by now.

John sighed, night-dark eyes flickering closed. "I've had tae fight before, but their weapons now, the silver ones, they sting. Worse than that uisge beatha Robert made that one time." A bark of a laugh coughed from him and Euan nodded at the memory of the burning taste of the alcohol.

A sigh shuddered from the older man and he drooped before continuing, "I have no the energy to heal this time. My time as Ceann-fine is up and..."

"No! No, you just need time. We'll leave here, you'll heal." The interruption was soft, broken, and John's eyes opened as he reached out with his right arm, wrapping his fingers tightly over the scar that marked Euan's shoulder, pulling him in close.

"No, not this time, Euan. Ye know it's so. The pack needs a strong leader, someone brave enough, fierce enough, loving enough to take them fae their homes and half way round the world. I cannae do it. I belong here. But you, you can take that New World and make it yours." John's voice cracked and trailed off in a soft gasp.

"John." The word was low, aching with pain and fear and love and Euan swallowed hard against the sting in his eyes and the way his throat had closed up so tight he feared he might never speak again.

"Euan..." John coughed, turning away to spit up dark fluid before he turned back to Euan, dropping his head to the ground, baring his the nape of his neck, the curve of his spine in symbolic submission. "Euan, as Ceann-fine of the Ranulf Clan, I ask ye for mercy."

Tears rolled unchecked down Euan's face as he wrapped his arms around the man who had become his leader, his friend, his second father. A sob shuddered free before he hauled in a hard breath and reached for the small scabbard held loosely in John's left hand.

"As Ceann-fine of the Ranulf Clan, I grant your request." Euan brought his arm round, sliding it between their bodies, pulling John in tight with his other arm. He felt the slight resistance as the blade met skin, before the sharp point slid between John's ribs, piercing deep and true. Euan felt it like a blow to his own chest, his breath stuttering and he swallowed hard against the sting of tears.

John shuddered gently, a slow breath easing out of him and Euan threw back his head and howled out the news of the Chieftain's death, the sacred silver blade falling unnoticed to the ground between them. Voices picked up the howl, echoing it through the trees, wolf and human cries joined in despair and grief. He felt Tris stir behind him, awoken by the sound of Euan's grief. Euan turned as a hand fell softly on his shoulder. Tris knelt behind him, eyes soft and wet with sympathetic tears.

He helped Euan rise, John's body cradled gently in his arms and followed as Euan paced steadily back to the remains of their haven. He headed for one of the small shelters not yet in flames, watching silently as Tris barely stopped to think when a soldier appeared in front of them, pulling the man forward and snapping his neck. Euan noticed Tris pause, caught him staring blankly at his hands and he tried to reassure him with a tight smile before he motioned him on with a nod. Other figures appeared out of the smoke and flames, dropping in behind Euan and Tris, those in human form darted off to each side, returning with armfuls of firewood.

The soldiers now seemed to be in retreat, perhaps finding it difficult to fight amongst the smoke they had created in their attempt to destroy the village. The wolves faded in and out of the smoke, slashing with claws or steel before disappearing back into the surrounding trees, or darting around the dwellings. Euan wondered whether they were trying to pull back and regroup for a more concerted attack, or whether their Captain had decided to try and hunt them down during the daylight. With their injured clansmen, they would be an easy target for men on horseback. He pulled Lachlan close and told him to try and hunt down as many soldiers as they could.

The sounds of battle faded away as Euan entered the small room, laying John's body gently down on the bed, hands resting on his chest. Robert came forward to slip an ornate dagger beneath the crossed palms, before he turned and tilted his head, baring his throat, the pulse of artery, to Euan. Ellen was next, her face blank, wet with the tears that rolled down over her cheeks, silent and unceasing. She covered John with a thin linen sheet, tucking it under his body then leant in to place a soft kiss to his forehead. The others left their firewood and gathered outside. Euan's head drooped, his body shuddering and Tris placed a gentle hand at the base of his spine. Euan flicked him a quick glance before he tossed a burning brand onto the roof.

Other brands followed, the flames licking greedily at the new source of fuel, spiralling high and bright into the night. A howl rose up again, the eerie sound echoing and repeating, as more voices picked it up. Euan turned to the remaining members of his clan, voice carrying as the howl died away.

"As Ceann-fine of the Ranulf Clan I ask ye, will ye follow?"

"Aye, we follow!" The call rang back from human throats, lupine voices barking sharply. Euan's head dipped, eyes closing as emotion flooded through him; the pain of loss, protectiveness for the clan that was now his, fear and anger and love all melding together in a giant ball that closed up his throat, sending his pulse swinging erratically and he wanted to drop to his knees and howl out his rage and he wanted to tear and rend and rip apart those who had broken his clan and he just wanted to curl up and hope it all just went away.

A strong hand slid up his spine, warm scent of autumn, rich with heather and bramble and Tris was there, Tris was right there. Euan spun round, one hand wrapping hard around Tris's throat, the other sinking into the wind-blown tangle of hair, pulling his head down hard. Mouths crashed together and Euan heaved Tris's breath into his lungs, sucked his taste into his mouth, biting and licking until his whole world tasted like, smelt like, felt like Tris.

He forced himself to pull back, stared at Tris's face, kiss-swollen lips, hazel eyes dark with emotion. He couldn't resist sliding his thumb up from the hollow of Tris's throat, over the racing pulse, slipping it over the slick, reddened bow of his lower lip. Lachlan's catcall pulled his attention away and Euan shifted back to being the new leader of this small clan. The group was split, bodies melting into the night, the injured paired with those that could help and in less than ten minutes the village was a ghost town, lit with the soft flickering flames as the soldiers searched in vain for the enemy that had vanished through their cordon, unseen and unheard.

Chapter 12
Finding the way

The group headed north and west, taking their time, hiding out during the day, giving the injured time to heal. The wounds caused by the silver coated blades festered and bled, sticky, dark and foul-smelling. They hunted for herbs and made poultices that smelt just about as bad to coat the wounds until the skin finally began to knit, pain fading. They took turns scouting ahead, and Tris finally began to get used to the fact that occasionally a large wolf would wander through their midst, brushing up against hips and arms.

He was also getting used to the way the world seemed to have become bigger, brighter, filled with scents and distractions. He wanted to know what it would look like as a wolf but Euan, when he managed to speak to him, kept putting him off, telling him to wait, that the full moon would make the first time easier.

Thinking about Euan hurt: the light-hearted man that had kidnapped him at sword point, the man that had flirted and joked with him as they made their way westwards had almost disappeared. The man that held him up against a damp cave wall in the dark, that kissed him like he was the end and the beginning, who made the world fall away in a shower of sparks, was gone completely.

Tris was beginning to wonder if he had imagined the entire night, that the way Euan had felt wrapped around him was a dream. But sometimes, as the small fires flickered in the dark, as they gathered together, waiting for the news of their departure to spread, for others to join them, Tris could feel Euan's gaze, felt it hot and heavy against his skin. Sometimes he awoke with the yellow scent of broom, the faintest hint of cherry blossom; the essence of spring, of Euan, heavy in the air with each breath he took.

He could see Euan talking, moving between each small group, making sure that the injured were healing, that everyone was fed. But Euan's stare jumped and flickered as it moved over him, never meeting his confused hazel gaze. Finally, Tris lost any patience he did have and after two days of this strange form of silent torture he sought out Ellen, wrapping her arm through his, slowing his steps so that they fell slightly behind the main group.

"Ellen, can I ask you about Euan? I need to help, I have to do something." Tris trailed off, unsure how to continue but Ellen hushed him, patting his arm as she let her gaze move to Euan.

"Euan's taking the loss of John hard, we all are, but now Euan thinks he has to be there for all of us. He's trying to be a good leader and it's going to tear him apart. It's easier for Meg and me, we've always been this way, we understand the pack mentality and we know that discipline is required, but we also know that... well I suppose play is the closest word we'll get to it... aye, that'll do. Euan needs to relax, he needs to play and I think ye are the only one that can help him with that."

Tris's mouth opened and closed as he processed Ellen's words. "But how... I mean, I can barely get Euan to look at me just now."

Ellen grinned, white and sharp and pulled Tris in close. "I think it's time ye got some education in how a pack works, and how best tae rile up our noble leader." Tris raised a curious eyebrow and settled into a slow walk beside the older woman.

"Now, ye probably have already noticed that we don't work quite like a normal Clan. A lot of the formalities are the same, we have a Ceann-fine, a Chieftain and he has his second. Just as in most communities the Chieftain's wife would have standing, but here my say is more absolute. I speak, or I did, with the same voice as John did."

Tris heard her breath hitch slightly and he moved to say that she didn't need to go any further if the matter was distressing. Ellen patted his arm, and gave a tremulous smile. "He should be remembered and we cannae do that if we remain silent. Now any children of the Ceann-fine would be expected to lead by example, but, until they prove themselves, all pack children are treated the same. They can come to any adult for advice. It may be that the child of the old Ceann-fine would take over, but I was never lucky enough to bear a male bairn to term."

Ellen smiled over at a golden tinged wolf running past. "Meg is the apple of my eye, but she's no ready to make any man a wife yet. There's too much of her father in her, that one. She says she's waiting for 'the one', that she wants what I had." Ellen smiled at the memories that statement brought back.

"So how will it work with Euan? Will he have to take a wife?" Something clenched inside Tris at the thought of that, and he swallowed down against the hard lump that formed in his chest.

"Bless you, child. Euan can barely keep his eyes from you. How he'd find time to court a lassie...." Ellen laughed, a light feminine sound that had others around them smiling too. "No, it's quite obvious to the rest of us that you two are mated, even if Euan is nae man enough yet to claim it. It could be that in time you might find a lassie that you could see bearing Euan's pups, but the role of the Ceannfine's mate is to nurture the pack as a whole, to educate, to smooth over difficulties between pack members. To my mind, ye're a great choice for Euan and I'm sure everyone else will come tae see that too. Now we just have to get Euan tae see what he's missing."

Ellen drew Tris closer again, their heads, dark and fair bending together. They spent the rest of the evening and well into the night talking and if Tris saw Euan casting them the occasional curious look, well, he just ignored it. It was about time their leader had a small taste of his own medicine.

They spent the next day in one of the small havens the clan had set up. Euan knew it wasn't safe, but Ellen had insisted. They were all in need of a proper rest and a proper meal, and as lead female, Ellen finally put her foot down and told Euan that the Clan was staying here for at least the next two days. She explained that a proper rest and a couple of decent meals would allow the injured to finish healing and give the others a chance to catch their breath and to relax, something vital for the mental health of the pack. Many of the small buildings were beginning to suffer from the Scottish weather, but there were enough habitable ones left and they piled in, five or six to a room. Lachlan, Meg and a couple of others disappeared out on a hunting trip and came back several hours later, dragging a small deer and a couple of rabbits.

The deer had been butchered and was now in various parts roasting, sizzling and filling the small glen with a delicious smell, the rabbits had made their way into a couple of cooking pots with what vegetables and roots as could be found, adding to the scent that was beginning to drive Tris mad.

He had been getting used to the way everything smelt; not stronger, but more defined, more of itself. He had even managed to stop himself from starting awake at every small animal sound in the night, now that it seemed like he could hear each time a hedgehog needed to pee. However, something had changed over the past day or so and Tris couldn't settle, his skin feeling both too big for his bones and yet stretched taut, itching and pulsing with each beat of his heart. Even his hair itched and hurt, tugging at the sensitive skin of his scalp. His teeth felt awkward in his mouth, like he suddenly had too many, or maybe not enough.

He took yet another wander around the edge of the clearing, looking over Meg's shoulder as she filled bowls with rabbit stew, poking at a haunch of venison, only to get his fingers slapped by Robert before Ellen finally snapped and pointed him in the direction of Euan.

"Go, afore ye drive us all demented."

Tris made it almost all the way across the small clearing before Euan spotted him, and Tris could tell the exact moment Euan noticed him approaching. His shoulders stiffened up and he jerked to his feet, taking a couple of steps off to one side before he stopped and nodded to Tris. He still didn't meet Tris's eyes, his gaze hovering somewhere over his shoulder.

"Euan, I need to talk to..."

"Not now Tris, I have tae go talk tae Ellen..."

"Euan, no!" Tris blinked at the growled demand that made its way out of his mouth, stomach clenching as a dark light flickered in Euan's eyes before the shutters came back down, blanking out his expression.

"Tris, I'm the Chieftain here, the clan's Ceann-fine, I have things I need tae do and I dinnae have time for whatever this is."

Another growl rumbled low and threatening in Tris's ears and Tris realised that it was coming from him, his upper lip curling back, flashing even, white teeth. Tris watched as Euan's eyes widened, then narrowed; staring transfixed as Euan paced slowly towards him, fingers curling at his sides. "I'm sorry Tristan, do ye have something tae say about that?"

The threat in Euan's voice was clear, and Tris soaked up Euan's undivided attention, moving sideways towards the trees, being careful not to drop his gaze or turn sideways. If Euan wanted Tris to submit he was going to have to make him. Tris could feel the blood racing hot through his veins, could feel his heart expand against his ribs. His skin twitched and rippled and he sucked in a breath as pain sank low into his bones. Another growl trickled out through clenched teeth, this one more in denial of the pain, confusion at his situation, but Euan's eyes flickered dark, his shoulders hunching forward.

Tris kept his eyes fixed on Euan's, watched as the green bled away, irises glinting gold in the pale light of the moon. *The moon!* Tris dared a quick glance upwards over Euan's shoulder, saw the moon hanging almost full behind the soft curve of a hill. As soon as he saw it, he realised what the tension inside him meant, why he had been feeling like his skin was not his own.

He had remembered Ellen's words, their conversation the other day and his lips curved in a sharp grin as it seemed her suggestions had been correct, her knowledge of Euan's reactions true. He taunted Euan once more, a toss of his head, a snort of derision, before turning his back, like Euan was nothing to him, not his leader, not the one he wanted, needed.

Without looking back, Tris slipped into the trees, pulling at laces, his clothes dropping unregarded to the ground behind him. He could feel his skin twitching and shuddering, the disturbing sense of bones shifting underneath. A howl was ripped from him, sound breaking and changing register as his throat and jaw shifted. Copper taste filled his mouth as his teeth lengthened and he dropped to the forest floor, spine arching and curling as the waves broke over and through him. And then he was other. His ears twitched and shifted at each small sound; the forest was layered in scents, the small faint trails of tiny creatures, the bigger trails of deer and human.

He heard the sounds of Euan's change, the wet sounds of flesh and the creaking pops of bones remaking themselves and a shudder rippled through his fur. It was strange, feeling the hair around his neck stand up, feeling his ears move. He twisted around to look at himself, could only see the length of his legs, slender and strong with muscle, the bunched muscle over his hips, the flag of his tail. He was so absorbed in himself that he almost didn't hear Euan's approach. His body jerked automatically, slipping sideways and turning so that Euan's pounce just grazed his hip instead of pinning him as he had intended.

Euan snarled, lips curling back to reveal a full complement of sharp fangs. Tris stood his ground, darting forward to nip at Euan's shoulder before dancing backwards. Tris's lips curled in the lupine equivalent of a smirk as Euan bristled, fur rising in a halo over his broad shoulders. Euan stalked forward again, legs stiff, head forward, a low rumble vibrating out of his chest. Tris faked another darting move to the left before running off to the right, twisting and turning his body through the trees.

It was surprisingly natural to move this way, his world view quickly adjusting to his new height, the way the world looked around him. His body contracted and stretched, paws moving swiftly over the fallen pine needles, crunching the skeletons of long discarded leaves. He paused for a short moment, senses working overtime as he was broadsided by the scents and sounds surrounding him. A deer stood somewhere over to his left, a rabbit had crossed the path just in front of him, Lachlan and Meg had passed this way earlier too, probably when they were hunting. Then he heard it, an almost eerie ululation, the high pitched sound raising the fur around his neck before the tone lowered and then faded out. His mate.

Chapter 13

Chased and Caught

Tris ran once more, delighting in the feel of his new muscles moving. He could hear the sounds of Euan's pursuit and he slowed his pace for a couple of steps, twisting to see where Euan was. Trying to use his sight like a human, instead of his wolf senses, meant that Tris gave Euan another chance to pounce, his broad head thumping into Tris's side, sending them tumbling through the undergrowth in a pile of snapping teeth and wayward limbs. It was sheer luck that Tris missed the fallen tree, rolling past the tangle of roots leaving Euan to get caught. Tris rolled to his feet, breath panting out of him and stalked towards Euan. His opponent was down and Tris's wolf wanted to take advantage, to try and assert his dominance, but just as Tris grew near, Euan untangled himself and snapped out at Tris.

Tris felt the pressure of teeth under his jaw, and half of him wanted to submit, to roll over and go belly up for Euan. But the stubborn, human side of him said that Euan needed to work harder, that he needed this chase, needed this time away from the worries of the pack. So Tris jerked himself free, sure that he had left a bunch of fur and possibly the taste of blood in Euan's sharp jaws, and darted off again into the trees. He managed to evade Euan for a little while, before the scent of fresh water brought his head round and he ran towards it.

He scrabbled to a sudden stop at the top of a waterfall, claws raking up the dirt and digging in lest he take a sudden, unexpected plummet into the large pool below. He turned, hearing Euan move out of the trees behind him. Euan was working solely on instinct now, needing to dominate, to get Tris to roll over and submit to him. He saw Tris and stalked forward, not taking time to wonder exactly why Tris had chosen that particular moment to stop and wait. A sudden leap found Euan passing over Tris, who had dropped, in an unexpectedly human move, flat-bellied, to the ground. Euan scrabbled for footing on the other side, only to find that there was not enough and he dropped into space.

Euan twisted as he fell, spotting the water, beginning to force the change. Tris was also focusing on his human self, picturing his other body, pushing the wolf back under, and could soon feel his body re-shape itself. He knew that he had probably, no make that definitely, overstepped the mark with that trick and he really wanted to be able to speak to Euan, to apologise, to explain.

Tris crawled over to the edge of the small cliff and watched as Euan hit the pool hard, disappearing beneath the dark water. He wait-ed, holding his breath, watching for a sign, waiting for a flash of pale skin. Panic rose in him, bringing him to his feet and he had just poised himself to dive in when Euan appeared, glistening in the moonlight as he broke the surface, face upturned to where Tris still stood on the cliff. Tris knew how he looked, silhouetted against the night sky and he held the pose for a moment before he raised his arms and dropped over the edge, slipping into the water like he was part selkie instead of part wolf.

Tris swam upwards and towards the edge of the pool, stopping once he could stand on the rocks at the bottom of the pool. Euan sur-faced next to him, hair slicked smooth and dark by the water, tiny beads trembling on those long lashes, glistening like dew on spider webs. Tris opened his mouth to speak, to make an attempt at apolo-gising but all that escaped was breath as Euan wrapped long fingers around his throat, the other hand tangling into the curls at the back of Tris's head.

A low growl rumbled out of Euan and then his mouth was hard on Tris's, teeth pulling at the tender skin of his lower lip, tongue slicking its way in hard and fast. Tris's vision started to swim and he swayed towards Euan, who released Tris's mouth and turned his attention to the tender skin of Tris's neck, sucking and biting until Tris was moan-ing his name and the tan skin was decorated with blossoming rosettes of purple and red, blood swelling heated under the skin's surface.

Tris watched, flushing, as Euan pulled back to survey the damage, a slow grin curling up the sides of kiss-stained lips. He felt Euan rub his thumb across the marks, the signs that would tell everyone that Tris was owned, that he belonged to Euan.

"Mine."

Tris's head lolled back, neck exposed, his hands resting gently on Euan's hips, thumbs rubbing up and down over the jut of bone. Hazel eyes blinked open slowly, focusing on the predatory stare that Euan was giving him.

"Yours." The word was soft, voice broken and rough with need and Tris leant harder into Euan, water-slicked chests sliding against each other. He could feel the small nubs of Euan's nipples, the skin pebbling with the cold of the water and the desire flaring low in his stomach.

Euan growled happily and Tris moaned at the feel of his teeth as he nipped at Tris's collarbone. He heard himself groan wantonly as Euan slid his hips up and against Tris's. Euan kept one hand wrapped over Tris's shoulder and neck, fingers constantly rubbing against the marks that were scattered over the tender skin as the other slid down and under the water, slipping over the firmness of chest, the soft ripples of Tris's stomach.

Tris jerked as Euan's fingers wrapped around the length of him, the water meaning that the friction was just on the right side of not enough and almost. He sought out Euan's mouth, licking gently at the plush lips, silently asking for entry, moaning happily as Euan slanted his mouth over his, tongues flirting back and forwards.

Then Euan's fingers were sliding backwards, a flush shivering its way up Tris's body as a finger applied pressure, sliding slowly inside. Tris couldn't help the curse that slipped free, a burning ache following Euan's finger. He wanted to pull away, but Euan kept his hand moving slowly over the length of Tris's shaft and his hips jerked forward, seeking pressure, friction. He felt the finger move inside of him, seeking something and then his vision flashed white, muscles he didn't know he had fluttering wildly, hips stuttering and Tris wondered if Euan was trying to kill him with pleasure.

He groaned, a soft sound of loss and despair as the finger moved away, leaving him empty and wanting, but then Euan was spinning him round in the water, pushing him up onto the bank. Tris fell forward onto this hands and knees, water streaming from him as he felt Euan push his legs further apart, making sure their bodies were steady on the uneven ground and then Tris felt something warm and wet lap at the small entrance, curling against the tight muscle. He bit back a cry as he realised exactly what Euan was doing, wanting to protest but the feeling was overwhelming, pleasure sparking through him from the wet pressure as Euan pressed his tongue harder against the sensitive flesh.

Euan worked him open slowly, curl of tongue and the firm pressure of a finger easing the saliva inside. As liquid started to seep from Tris's untouched cock, Euan gathered it on his fingers and fed it back into Tris, slicking him further, making him moan with each small caress over the head of his shaft.

He felt Euan crawl out of the water behind him, pushing him further up onto the grass as Euan covered his body with his own. Euan's other hand curled around his chest, hand pressed firmly over the rise of Tris's pectoral muscle, holding him in place as he worked the now slick finger rapidly in and out. "Euan, please... I need... you have to... Euan.... oh..." The last word slipped away on a moan as Euan slid yet another finger inside and Tris felt so full and he wanted so much and all he could do was plead and beg.

"Who d'ye belong to Tris? Tell me." And Euan was thrusting those clever fingers in and out and it was all Tris could do to haul in air and gasp it out.

"Yours, Euan's, yours... oh God... please... yours..."

Then the fingers were pulling away again and Tris was bereft for a brief moment before Euan moved forward, pushing against him, body moving slick and easy and there was pressure and heat and Tris was so full, the world spinning off around him. Euan leant back, pulling Tris up against his chest, pressing an open mouth to the curve of his neck and the feelings coalesced into the two points of heat and pressure that were Euan's hard cock inside him and Euan's mouth on his neck. Euan moved against him, one hand still bracing his chest, the other pressed low against his stomach as if to feel himself inside. Tris groaned, tilting his hips back towards Euan. All of a sudden it was right there, the world went white and Tris's orgasm shuddered through him and out, every muscle tightening, clenching around

Euan and pulling him along with Tris.

Tris came back to himself slowly, the chill of the remaining water against his skin, the heat of Euan's body against the length of his spine, and the soft caress of Euan's mouth over the nape of his neck. A soft hum of pleasure slipped out before it was broken off by a shiver. Euan slid out carefully, placing a soft kiss to the base of Tris's spine before he moved away, rising to stand nude and proud on the bank. Tris rolled onto his back, enjoying the view for a long moment before beginning to push himself up.

"Shift your arse, Tris, I can't be waiting on ye all night." Tris pulled himself up and moved towards Euan, seeing the smirk curling up the side of his mouth, finally seeing the Euan that had been missing the last couple of days, hidden under the new Chieftain. Dimples appeared as Tris smiled, broad and sated.

"Aye, sir."

Euan's palm swung low, cracking against the firm muscle of Tris's thigh in a playful swat. "Aye, dinnae forget that."

Tris's fingers moved up to trace the circlet of bruises that trailed in shades of plum and cherry across his throat and collarbones. "I don't think I can." His voice deepened and his head lowered as he peeked at Euan through his lashes.

Euan made a strange sound, a cross between a moan and a sigh, and pulled Tris in close, lips tracing over his marks of possession. Tris let his head fall back, throat bared in tempting submission.

"Tha gaol agam ort." The words slipped out of Euan's mouth, whispered against Tris's ear and even though they were not in English, Tris knew exactly what Euan meant.

"Me too."

The sun was rising, painting the sky in shades of peach and gold before they made it back to the encampment.

The clan had been watching the supplies being taken on board, the many and varied things that would support their small group as they travelled so far from their homes. They all knew that they could no longer remain here, the dramatically carved hills, the gentle spread of forest, the clear lochs and rivers were no longer safe for them. But it was such a big step, to take everything they had, everything they were, and to trust it all to this fragile creation of wood and rope. To follow the setting sun to the new world.

Euan watched the gulls as they spiralled over the waves, dipping out of sight behind the spars, the vast sweep of sail. He felt warm fingers wrap around his, a brief caress, hidden between their bodies and he turned to Tris, losing himself again in the hazel depths of his eyes. Tris smiled down at him and Euan could scent the reassurance, the calm excitement that Tris felt. He watched Tris's eyes darken, trembled at the subtle flare of desire, quickly hidden. And he knew that no matter how far he went, he took his home with him, as long as Tris was there.

A call rang out, breaking the intimacy and the two men turned to see the rest of their clan, their makeshift family, collect the last of the belongings and head towards the slender bridge between land and ship, past and future. Ellen and Meg led the way, the others followed on and it was Tris's turn to feel the brush of Euan's fingers. He returned the gesture with a dimpled grin. They paused to let a young couple board in front of them, the man slim and pale, strawberry blond hair bright in the sunshine. The girl followed after, her features a delicate, feminine version of what was obviously her brother. She watched her brother bound ahead, lithe and steady across the swaying boards and began to make her own crossing. Her brother called out a reassurance and the girl dared a glance upwards, then a foot landed awkwardly, fear and panic slicing through the air.

Euan was reaching out a hand, almost before he realised, as the young girl slipped, wrapping it tight around the fragile bones of her wrist. He could feel Tris move swiftly behind him, an arm swinging round to add extra support, pulling the woman back from the edge of the wooden strip, supporting her gently until she was balanced and moving forwards, up onto the deck of the ship.

She paused there at the top, and reached out to Euan, saying softly, "Thank you, Sir." A gust of wind played with her headscarf, teasing pale blonde strands out from under it, blowing them across her face. She tucked them back as Euan stared, taken by her fragile beauty. Tris laughed softly beside him. He pulled Euan close and whispered in his ear, "Thinking of enlarging the clan already? Do you think Meg would appreciate another pretty blonde?"

Euan turned and smacked at Tristan's arm. "Jealous, leannan? And, no, I'm sure if Meg wants a gift, she can get her ain. Mind you...."

Tris pouted gently and Euan grinned and pushed him further along the railing, leaning into the hard length of the body beside him as they watched the sailors pull in the rope bridge, the small figures of the dock workers below unwinding ropes, which snaked down into the dark water that rose and fell like a heartbeat, cradling the vessel. Cries rang out across the ship, canvas billowed and cracked as the wind took it and with a myriad of creaks and yells the ship slipped away from the land.

Euan blinked as his home blurred in his vision, the smell of salt strong in his nose instead of the familiar bite of damp green, sharp yellow broom, fresh cold water. His eyes fell closed and he tried to fix a memory in his head but then there it was – pale purple heather, the deeper stain of bramble, dark and green and home and he opened his eyes and smiled at Tris, who turned as Ellen slipped her arm through his, and twitched away as Meg tried to ruffle his hair. Together, they turned their faces towards the west.

About the Author

Kailin Morgan has always been an avid reader. She discovered goth and industrial music and vampires and werewolves at about the same time. As part of the alternative subculture, she has always been open to different fashions, tattoos and piercings and self-expression. She rediscovered the love of writing through fan-fiction and has since quickly become addicted to the thrill of discovering new characters. Although most of her writing is m/m, she also loves writing strong female characters. Her writing tends towards fantasy, dealing with gods and monsters, but she loves to place them into everyday settings and see what happens. Now a slave to the muse, Kailin looks forward to spending many hours hiding from the Scottish weather, hunched over her laptop, typing feverishly whilst existing solely on caffeine.

Works by Morgan Kailin

Stone Cold Heart
Judge Not
Strange Hospitality
Underneath It All
Forever After

Saint of the Sinners
Red and the Wolf

His Highland Wolf

About the Publisher

ForbiddenFiction.com is a publisher devoted to writing that breaks the boundaries of original erotic fiction. Our stories combine intense sexuality with quality writing. Stories at ForbiddenFiction.com not only arouse readers through sensations, but also engage them emotionally and mentally through storytelling as well-crafted as the sex is hot.

ForbiddenFiction.com is also designed to be a social reading environment. You'll have fun even if just reading the latest post each day, yet you will have the chance for so much more. Readers and authors can be part of ongoing discussions of specific works and individual authors as well as more general topics.

Sign up for a FREE Membership today at ForbiddenFiction.com